MW01139179

Liberation in the East

CHIP MARTIN grew up in California and since the early 1970s has lived in London. He has edited magazines, taught writing at Harvard and lectured on literature for the British Council. As Stoddard Martin he is author of several books on Romanticism and Modernism, including *Wagner to the Waste Land* and *The Sayings of Friedrich Nietzsche*. His fiction includes *A Revolution of the Sun*, *A School of London* and *The Undead*.

The photograph on this cover was taken by Aliki Roussin. The masks were made by Philippa Stockley.

Chip Martin

Liberation in the East

a romance

by Chip Martin

Starhaven

First edition, 100 copies
signed by the author

No. **97**

Starhaven
Box 2573, La Jolla, CA 92038, USA
in UK, C/o 42 Frognal, London NW3 6AG
Tel: 020 7435 8724
email: starhaven@aesthesia.co.uk

Designed and set in Excelsior by John Mallinson.
Printed on vellum paper and bound by
CPI Copyspeed, 38 Ballard's Lane, London N3 2BJ.

for A.L., K.T. and E.H.

I.

The Lady Lecturer

'Why is it, do you think, that English people abroad go so
very queer – so ultra-English – incredible! – and at the
same time so perfectly impossible?... As for their sexual
behaviour... all flagrant, quite unabashed – under the
cover of this fanatical Englishness.'

— D. H. Lawrence, *Aaron's Rod*

Geraldine Scott spoke with the pent-up enthusiasm of a
woman returning to her old school – possibly to lecture the
girls on how to achieve a career as exemplary as hers. Few Poles
had noticed her when she'd come to their country a decade
before as part of a feminist tour sponsored by the British
Council. But under the new conditions of life in the East, it was
imperative to act as if any Westerner returning were a long-
standing comrade.

Geraldine had been wary of Poland in the heady days of
martial law, but now that she was here as glamorous lecturer and
author, the *film noir* spirit-of-place took on a story-book aura for
her. Things she had feared during the old régime seemed almost
exotic. Over lunch with her hosts from the Warsaw Philological
Institute, she reminisced about her phone having been tapped as
if it were a station of the cross. She even defended the old system
as being efficient, a thing no Westerner would have dared at a
time when Solidarity members were having their testicles
zapped for *samizdat* publications of *1984*.

The young man assigned to guide Geraldine was called Krzysztof Robiński. Krzysztof tried not to be annoyed at the tone these Westerners took; he merely ferried this one around to her appointments in his diminutive Polski Fiat. Professor Scott had recently written a novel to complement her list of articles and a monograph on 'The Myth of the Virgin and Whore in Literature, Drama and Film'. The novel was being puffed; it had a Polish student in it, stage-Pole as it were: polite, eager to please, somewhat oppressed. This is what had persuaded the powers-that-be that it might be a good wheeze to send the lady back to 'old haunts'. She could be their star turn at a showcase conference near Kraków; *en route* she could do readings and all-purpose ambassadressing. – Western officials were keen on things like this now in the East, since the changes had come.

First stop was dinner and a reading at the Writers' Guild. Made up mostly of hacks approved of in Party days, this group was falling all over itself now to be ingratiating to 'old friends from the West'. Krzysztof delivered Geraldine to their restored Hanseatic headquarters on a corner of the Palace Square; there she was also scheduled to spend the night. Led up eighty stairs to the highest garret, she opened a window to let out musty air and found herself almost able to touch the tip of the crown of Sigismundo III on his pillar. Though she didn't know it, this was one of the premier views in Warsaw. You could see the 18th century palace, now fully rebuilt, and the Wisła, Poland's 'backbone', flowing below the escarpment on which it stood. From the writers' point of view, it was superior to and more politically correct than the alternative: the Stalinist Palace of Kultur out the windows of the 'American Palace of Culture' (Marriott Hotel) across town. But when Krzysztof arrived in the morning to collect her, the lady professor complained:

'Those bloody bells! They went on all night. Every quarter of an hour!'

Krzysztof knew that if he had stayed in a place so historic he would have been unable to sleep. The bells of the cathedrals and great Catholic churches of Warsaw, which had done so much to pry off the dead hand of Brezhnevian bureaucracy, were music to the ears of a patriotic Pole. He would have been dozy in the morning, true: like the Indians or Mexicans Westerners referred to when making comparisons about the laid-backness of the East. But then Krzysztof Robiński had no ambition to be geared up to the level of tension of an English lecturer arriving for her royal progress through his newly 'liberated' land.

Professor Scott was not quite what he had envisioned from the photographs he and his pert little girlfriend Agnieszka had pinned up at the Institute to announce her reading. In person she was taller and blonder, her hair blacker at the roots, her bones big. She looked very English, her face sharper than a Pole's or a German's, the eyes more animated, the whole aspect more energized. In a way, she was slightly alarming to look at: more intensely *there* than you might have guessed from her work, which had a circumambulatory quality about it, like Virginia Woolf's. All that stuff about 'the essential English lyricism' and 'gentle harmonies of our pastoral ideal' made her seem 'half in love with easeful death', as old Communist teachers used to say was typical of Western decadence.

But she didn't look decadent. And her speaking-voice was subtle even as it complained. Krzysztof had to ask her to repeat what she'd said. ('The balls kept me awake all night'? No, that couldn't have been it.) And later at lunch when she cast words his direction over a colleague, he felt compelled to answer, 'Could you repeat, please? I think I am going a bit deaf.' He was not going deaf, of course, not at age twenty-two; he just thought it tactful to say so. He'd seen her rubbing her temples during the morning's question-and-answer session and knew she was feeling the twitches and aches all Westerners seemed to suffer from on arriving here. What was it? the coffee? low-pressure in the air? Did they bring neurosis with them, or did it only flare up when they realized they were stuck for days in a place which must have seemed purgatory to them?

It was not paradise for Poles either, Krzysztof reflected; especially not those who had spent time in the West, as he had. But it was theirs, and they had to make the most of it – the ones who had not been so selfish, or enterprising, as to have escaped entirely. That's why he didn't encourage her to go on with her complaints about the water, etc. once they'd finished their long Polish lunch and were safely back into his little machine.

He deposited her at the Marriott for an appointment with a man from the World Bank. Now why should she have wanted to meet with a man from the World Bank? He didn't ask. He simply waited in the glitter of the café on the *rez-de-chaussée* of the 'American Palace of Culture' and, to pass time, sketched a young woman playing violin in the string trio there.

She seemed new at her job and not very assured. *Eine Kleine Nachtmusik* came out as if the music itself had been written in the language of the Nazis. Was it pathetic? Would Poland seem pathetic to his Western guest? The girl looked as fashionable as she could in a frock her mother had sewn. All Polish girls wore frocks their mothers had sewn, even when they were nearly grown. It was touching but in contrast to Western style subtly humiliating... Must've come from Łódź or some grey place like that. Her mother doubtless worked in some textile mill there – one of the many going bust now.

Western businessmen swirled around neo-Vienna shaking their heads about it: 'Take at least ten years, maybe twenty... Would've been better if the whole place'd been blown up in the War, have to be re-tooled now entirely. Nothin' to salvage; smash 'em down; start from scratch... Damn state-owned factories! can't even compete with the Malaysians in t-shirts.'

At last, Professor Scott resurfaced:

'I hope I haven't kept you waiting,' she smiled, trying to glimpse what he had drawn.

'Not at all!' he replied, shutting his notebook, though it had been enough time to sketch the young woman from three different angles. 'Shall we go?'

Out the revolving doors... A lackey in blue uniform ushered the grand lady into the Polski Fiat as if it were a Mercedes. Geraldine neglected to give him a tip. Does she expect me to do it, Krzysztof wondered, calculating that his grant was worth £70 a month while her salary must have been at least £3000. Shrugging, he gave the man 5,000 zł. and started up.

At Aleje Jerozolimskie (Jerusalem Street), he stopped for an old Russian lady to cross. Swaying from side to side on swollen ankles, she clutched a frayed bag in swollen hands. Her face was buried in an overcoat so tight that it looked like a sausage-skin. Was she living or dying? – Professor Scott failed to notice. She was busy trying to entertain him by imitating some oddity of speech used by the Man from the Bank.

They were on the road then, for the big conference on English studies in Eastern universities. Since the changes had come, this kind of event had burgeoned, thanks to multinational 'orgs' like the Bank. That's why Geraldine had gone to see the Man, she disclosed. Locals had been left to make the arrangements.

'I wonder what it'll be like,' she mused, her ears ringing still with the Man's remark, 'They couldn't organise a piss-up in a brewery'. – Now why had he said that, and to her of all people? Did he think her clubbable into his code of John Majorite chauvinism? Feeling affronted on behalf of 'the natives', Geraldine made a point of trying to befriend her driver as they escaped the Warsaw suburbs.

'The Krakówians are in charge,' Krzysztof observed, though not sure she required an answer. 'They have a great rivalry with us here in Warsaw, so we don't know what to expect.'

'They've invited some big guns,' Geraldine mused, as if she were a metaphoric pea-shooter.

'Yes, and it's all about your English.'

Half-trying for irony, he added:

'Your language and literature are all the rage now.'

'The new Latin.'

'Please?'

'As the Roman language became the *lingua franca* throughout Europe in the Dark Ages, so the Anglo-Saxon will become for the world in a future in which our old empires vanish.'

She sounded like a book. Was she preparing her talk? She was meant to speak at the first session. I'll bet she's nervous, Krzysztof thought and surprised himself by wondering what her body must feel like on the inside as she worked up to such an exposure.

'After my speech I hope to take it easy,' she confessed, leaning her straw-coloured hair against a window.

The Mazowian plain passed. After Warsaw, it seemed almost familiar to her. Nature everywhere belongs to everyone, she thought and began to be soothed.

It was early spring here; all was yellow and green. Not so yellow and green as in London, but... Actually, the earth seemed slightly infertile to her. Still, it was warm. And there were genuine peasants out working the potato fields and farm boys lounging in the long grasses under a midday sun.

Before Kraków, it grew hilly – gentle hills, 'rolling' as an American might say. It seemed cleaner and more prosperous than the sector they'd come from.

'This was the Austrian part, wasn't it?'

'Please?'

'The Austrian sector, during the Partitions. One can tell really. It's so much more – *gemütlich*, isn't it?'

She gazed through nostalgic, neo-imperialistic eyes at a district once governed from elegant Vienna, not grim Petrograd. So would Poznań and Wrocław have pleased her even better, Krzysztof thought crossly, everything there having been ordered by Bismarck from Berlin?

'My dear Poland!' he sighed inwardly, but he said: 'Didn't one of your famous authors write, "History is a nightmare from which I wish I could awake"?'

'Sorry?'

'It's nothing,' he murmured, embarrassed.

But Geraldine Scott seemed to register a human, even intellectual quality in her driver then. 'He was Irish,' she answered. 'And not quite "one of ours". James Joyce.'

✳

'Recognising the stories that haunt a culture,' she intoned from the stage of a modernist auditorium at the conference centre on the Oświęcim side of Kraków; and on the phrase Krzysztof's mind wandered. Nor in wandering was it alone. There had been no coffee after lunch in the castle which made up the other part of the compound; so the lady lecturers from the Catholic

6

University of Lublin, who'd had to catch a train at six a.m. to get there, were fighting to keep their eyes open.

Krzysztof's own mental travel took the form of contemplating the medium, not the message. Professor Scott had just one feature in common with the middle-aged women who dominated the language institutes of the East: width in hip. Otherwise her features were Western and slim, as if out of some old Flemish painting. Idealism and zeal seemed to radiate from them, suggesting she was not trying to do what she did, she just *did*: she just *was*, the state of the art – of Western culture and civility at that moment in time, its attainment in discourse, befriending but tough-minded.

She was authority, he imagined sleepily. Yet when she smiled, she turned into an amused girl. Remote on the platform, she was nonetheless down-to-earth in her full skirt and pear-bottomed shape. She seemed more normal, ironically, than she had in informal chat; he wanted to draw her, but she was too far away. – Was she wearing blue stockings? No: they were mauve. And she was more than just a British *femme savante*: she was an embodiment of 'mental-spiritual attainment' (the phrase came from one of his teachers at Pittsburgh during his six months' exchange there), also of that great British word and concept *class*.

Yet she criticized class-distinction. What a luxury, he thought, seeing as she came from it. Geraldine Scott was what all these middle-aged Polish ladies wished they could be, with their tales of castles in Ukraina or Litwa, now all gone with the wind. Dispossessed for centuries, they could hardly afford to self-mock. She, on the other hand, could cast off her status quite blithely, or appear to... Must have given an intoxicating sense of power, he thought. Maybe it was what allowed her to turn her lecture into a re-rationale for Marx – a thing Polish docents would never dare do.

After her lecture, he sat on a bench in a courtyard studying the sun as it came through the leaves. The leaves were no more than green shoots yet. The sun was pale still, simmering through a cool haze up from the Wisła.

The conference centre was on a palisade at the edge of a

forest, situated on the last stretch of flat land before hills rose up into the Tatras Mountains. It was lovely here. The birds adored it. Krzysztof had heard a lark and a woodpecker, a pheasant and countless sparrows in the dawn chorus – no cawing rooks such as terrorized smaller birds in 'the Russian sector'. On the other hand, the centre had been built as a spa for the SS by Hans Frank and completed by the Party just before martial law; that was why the top of the hill was occupied by this modular, East Berlin-ish *aula* and the bottom by a neo-Nürnburg sort of thing. Nothing was perfect in Poland, not even here. Still, it could not stop the bird song. And Krzysztof believed he was happier than he could have been as an *émigré* in Chicago or even Hammersmith.

But what would her reaction be, he found himself wondering when the next plenary session broke up (something incomprehensible about linguistics) and she emerged into the sun and brushed past him.

'Enjoying yourself?' she inquired airily.

It sounded rhetorical. Still, it was enough to make him follow her into the one of several seminars by Polish colleagues she elected to attend after the break.

This was led with a paper by a young lady from Łódź. Pinched, be-spectacled, she had chosen as her subject Eastern European totalitarianism in recent Western drama. Foreigners were eager for such things. To hear about horrors without having to experience them was part of the excitement of coming east. Like the nostalgia Geraldine had expressed for her phone being tapped, it gave a brief, vicarious attachment to the nasty times they'd read about in spy-thrillers.

For Polish people, of course, it was yesterday's news. And since the medium was neither attractive nor significant-looking, Krzysztof let his eyelids droop.

The words came out – sharp, angular, monotonous. After a time, he found himself sitting bolt upright to listen to them. Something in the voice he could not quite place… And why amid all this talk about 'signified' and 'signifier' did no one pay attention to the music of speech?

Half-dreaming still, Krzysztof imagined a long, sensual talk with Professor Scott about it on the road back to Warsaw. He would say – but what *could* he say? He had never learned any language in which to talk about music: not the music of a remarkable voice. It all had to do with the rises and falls, the intervals between them, the ways in which different parts of a sentence or paragraph were modulated, the progress to and from climaxes. Such things interested him more than mere words. But would they interest her too?

After the session, she was surrounded by Polish colleagues eager for chat. They all wanted tickets to London and, by buttering her up, hoped to get a free bed or bursary. So Krzysztof sauntered back to the courtyard where he'd listened to the bird song and now sat listening again, imagining himself as Chopin in Łazienki Park back in Warsaw.

Of course he was neither tubercular nor blessed with the composer's talent for turning sound into form, and for a time he felt oddly ashamed. There was no genius in him, not for anything really. But though he could *make* nothing out of these sounds, he could enjoy them at least. And wasn't it just the most inarticulate sensations that were the most profoundly moving?

Professor Scott strolled up from the castle, trailed by her court of admirers. From time to time, she nodded to this one or that in the manner of Christ among his apostles or the Queen on walkabout. Did it make him jealous? Could she see this in his eye? Is it why she made a point of sitting next to him an hour later, down in the audience off of the platform, for the afternoon's session?

'You'll like this,' she murmured as if he were just some free-and-easy lad out for a lark.

What Krzysztof was meant to like was an antique Englishman with polished skull, white wisps on the side and a pair of half-glasses sliding down a crooked nose. His shirt was striped, his suit tweed, his tie bowed, his boots buttoned and of Edwardian cut. 'A true English eccentric,' Geraldine whispered. Krzysztof thought he could feel her body billowing out under a receptive tension.

Leaning against his lectern, the 'eccentric' invoked a tradition of out of Dickens or *Punch*. Professor Twitch he was named, and

9

his subject was 'The Ideology of the Early Fabian Society and Future of Democratic Socialism'. All Westerners seemed to want to talk about things like that. Polish colleagues grew restive.

So what was Twitch's point? To 'amuse on a hot afternoon', he declared; to preach entertaining, effective but low-key. He had readied himself, he confessed, by drinking a beer in the sun. Perhaps as a result, his 'lecture' evolved into little more than a reading of letters by well-heeled socialists of the 1890s satirizing their less well-known brethren.

So was this the sort of thing the English liked?

Krzysztof's mind returned to the previous evening in the 'cave' beneath the castle where this same Professor had complained like a baby when his minders had tried to take him home. He had wanted to stay drinking with the younger Polish colleagues, especially the women or – as he'd put it – 'girls'. Now in his speech he referred to the sexual exploits of his youth:

'I lied in good Anglo-Saxon monosyllables. And so did they!'

So was *this* what the Westerners wanted? amusing lies?

Under her breath, Professor Scott muttered 'politically incorrect', but Krzysztof could see she forgave it in a man of sixty. Was she amused too by the matador tightness of his trousers? a tactic, or perhaps advert, which, because of his age, an observer might dismiss as no more than a sign of an old man's forgetfulness, like egg-stain on a waistcoat or unbuttoned flies?

Krzysztof was not quite yet aware of a disgruntlement rising. It rumbled down below the bird song, as it were: like an ominous preview in the lower keys of a storm about to burst up through the octaves. Being superficially all a stage-Pole was meant to be, he kept his expression in cheerful upper notes. Professor Scott got a smile each time she blessed him with one of her perceptions. He even let her strike up a conspiratorial intimacy with him, as if he didn't recognize her attentions as a temporary mask – an entirely Platonic brushing-up against a younger man by a woman of thirty-five. – Or was it forty?

He was sufficiently under her spell that he'd wound himself up to something like her receptive tension by the time she settled beside him for the main event of the conference, the last plenary session.

The speaker this time was a noted Slavic *émigré* who'd once been in a gulag but still was known as a demi-Marxist – this despite, or possibly because of, years of sipping cappuccino in Harvard Square. Unlike with Twitch, the medium was not the message. Lean-necked and be-stubbled, this exhibit wore clothes that looked like they might have been new in the '60s or bought in some grim town like Łódź. All Voice as it seemed, he had come to inform his 'Post-Communist' brethren that the ideological trends of recent decades were over. Deconstruction, pure Theory, even Feminism had given way to what he entitled 'Neo-Pragmatism, Post-Modernism and the Politics of Culture'.

'During centuries of Dissociation of Sensibility,' he intoned, 'Art, Religion and Sexuality were driven from the Public Realm into arenas of Private Consciousness. Only there could impulses to the Mystic, the Fantastic and the Irrational be exercized. Because these Transcendental Urges were separated off as it were, they operated as a Critique of Experience at large, much of which came to be occupied by a Degraded Language of Reason.'

Geraldine smiled. So was this the sort of thing supposed to get your brain going, this talking in Capital Letters?

Krzysztof concentrated the more in order not to seem like a dunce on the road back to Warsaw.

'Freedom, Sensuality and Happiness are what True Culture is partisan for. But these have become complicit in our era with a dominant Utilitarianism. Art, Sex and Religion must declare themselves compromised now, even when trying to articulate their True Natures. Whereas Culture was once a refuge in which Utility and Reason might be escaped, it has become a locus of the trouble – perhaps the heart of our troubles – as matters of Individual Identity and Desire become the Essence of Conflict.'

For a moment, concentrating, Krzyzstof felt like some revelation was at hand. The words were so pregnant that his brain almost hurt. Yet here was a music too – not so much of sound as idea. And for the first time in his experience, he glimpsed how the realms of the mind might be as exciting as a vision in nature or of a beautiful girl.

'The terrain of Culture is now occupied territory, just like

11

Politics or Economics.' ('What areas of human activity are *not*?' Geraldine wrote on the edge of Krzysztof's notebook, an act of intimacy increasing his tension more.) 'Anarchy and Autocracy, the Market and Metaphysics cheek-by-jowl, shopping-malls as neo-Egyptian palaces... Yet this kind of play must to be counteracted by some Unified Faith: some coherent Subjectivity to exist alongside the discontinuous, eclectic forms we have taken on. Though we all are in some sense con-men operating by a Nietzschean *Wille-zur-Macht*, still we cry out for some Collective Ideal to legitimate our actions. So there is conflict between what we do and what we say we do; between Culture as Utility and Culture as Transcendence; between political paeans to God and country and having our hands in the till.'

Geraldine wrote: 'What about powers and capacities that are intrinsically morbid?' But by this time her thought was confined to her own notebook, the moment for flirtation having apparently passed.

Did she think her reactions too deep for a mere Polish lad? Is that why she now did not even notice him now reading over her shoulder? Was this all he could hope for from her kind ever: the status of some bimbo to a magnate?

Came the questions and answers:

'What about viewing culture as historical movement?' a young Polish colleague asked. 'It deconstructs blockages and is never static but at the same time is never wholly unifying.'

Krzysztof was surprised at the weight of these words. Had everyone's intellect caught fire suddenly? Could a conference like this become more than a mere prancing of egos? Had he spent so long in the low cynicism of students that people like Geraldine were right to patronize him?

Someone else, one of the decorous ladies from Lublin, spoke of 'restoration of older values of God and Christianity': another predictable response in the new East, especially given the 'God is Dead' *Zeitgeist* the Voice had noted.

Finally, a young women lecturer – the same who had given the paper on totalitarianism in Western drama – cried out: 'But what's going to happen to *me*?'

The room hushed. Faces turned.

Fiercely, she added: 'It seemed that a few years ago your "Post-Modernism" was going to be post-Communism and we were all going to feel better. But now I'm beginning to feel worse. And I don't just speak for myself.'

Grumbles commenced. Soon a familiar Eastern discontent was let loose. And before long the session had declined into cries, objurgations, contradictions, suppressed furies, until all the Voice could conclude was:

'In a crucial way, you are in transition here. Perhaps we all are, West now like East, as we approach our *fin-de-siècle*.'

'*Fin-de-millennium*,' Geraldine corrected.

But the girl who had started it cried, '*Fin-du-globe!*' And one of the polite Catholics docents rose to defend 'our lady guest' with a zest which suggested that the pertinacious creature was little more than the moral equivalent of some rabid wild dog.

✳

But what on earth was she thinking? a twenty year-old Polish lad and she, at forty, one of the youngest full professors of Eng Lit in Britain? She had never contemplated such a thing in London, or anywhere else for that matter. Her friends had come to think of her as frigid. Her ex live-in man, Leoline Hooper, had turned up on her doorstep now and then when one of his ladies got bored with his negligent ways; but though she had let him in once or twice, Geraldine had not had sex with him since the third time she'd caught him being unfaithful, pathetic man! So what was she imagining on the road back from Kraków? Was it as low and as bad as West German businessmen crossing the border into Czechoslovakia to have the girl of their choice for one-tenth of the cost back in Munich?

The weather was grim by the time they reached Warsaw: more like the dead-end of winter than middle of spring. The trees on the approach road looked nearly bare still: black and slick under a chilling drizzle. Grey road, dull cars, dirty Central Station… Geraldine hurried into the Marriott for her debriefing with the Man from the Bank. After that, she'd be finished with obligations and they could have fun, she told Krzysztof.

Did he look abashed? – He started off to the LOT building to wait for her in the O'Hare Pub. 'Have anything you want,' she heard herself call after his departing torso; 'I'll pay!' Then she rushed through her meeting with *hauteur* and impatience before refitting her mask and going to find him.

Her boldness was elating. She felt a rush of blood up the neck as on the first time she'd delivered a paper to an MLA conference – a critical moment in her career carrying her forward to an American job, prestigious publication and articles about her before she'd reached an age when women colleagues were contemplating their first pregnancies. But now she ached to be out of the fishbowls of London and academe. Under such scrutiny as she was, her physical being felt stifled.

Not that this place evoked fertility – far from it. Physical flourishing was the last thing you might think of gazing out the plate-glass behind which Krzysztof sat over the remains of an American breakfast. Vendors on curbside, pickpockets from the station across Jerusalem Street, the aggressive and sad from Belarus or further east bearing all the cheap goods they could hawk – it was as bad or worse than the worst of America: say, Newark, New Jersey. But this was central Warsaw! the capital city! the heart of the nation in terms of wealth!

Over the ruck rose one exotic skyscraper. The Stalinist Palace of Kultur had not yet been dismantled, Krzysztof explained, as many Poles wished.

'Let's go and see it!' Geraldine cried out in her new *let's have fun!* attitude.

'In this weather?'

'Darling boy, weather is of no importance to an Englishwoman on her day off. You must show me everything!'

'There are twelve buildings just like it in Moscow,' he added to dampen her interest; but it was no use.

They rode a lift to the top of the thirty-three stories. Below them the city spread out in uniform grey blocks under a leaden sky. Even in the face of this, Geraldine was determined to enthuse. The sands were flowing: one had to take *fun* as one could, at least one at her point in the hour-glass and as desperate as she felt.

Against a frigid wind, they gazed out. A balcony ran along four sides of the tower, like the viewing platform at the Tour Eiffel or Empire State Building. As in those places, graffiti abounded: teenagers' names, the logos of rock bands, vaginae and phalloi in comic couplings. Depressing that the East should have produced nothing better than this, she thought but resisted the temptation to state.

Holding her arms tight over her breasts, she shifted closer to Krzysztof for warmth. He went rigid. Nothing was said.

'What next, O guide?' she murmured jocularly, putting a hand through his arm and adopting the tone of a fascinated student as he took her down and around the vast Russian market which spread out like the remains of an explosion at the Palace's base.

They crossed a broad central boulevard and wound through blocks of massive, silent government buildings into a great square bounded by hotels.

'Should I book a room in one of these?'

The arm tightened.

'We can decide later,' she added to mitigate embarrassment. 'I'm not tired yet.' (A complete lie.) 'Show me what you call the Old Town.'

So they crossed to the Great Theatre and passed from grey, bland space into narrowing streets with pastel stucco constructions in odd, quaint shapes. These she recognized. It was the district where she had slept her first night. As if recognizing some *faux pas* then, she murmured:

'It's so precious, and clean! Reminds me of Denmark.'

A Disneyland Denmark, she neglected to add: a Polish urban theme park of a more picturesque past, which, she suspected, was little more than imaginary. But Krzysztof seemed proud of it.

He ducked her in doorways of three or four churches: poor cousins to the baroque magnificences of Munich. On shop fronts and in the cobbled square, *trompes d'oeil* were freshly painted. Gilded cupidons and all manner of vulgar ornamentation seemed to evoke splendour to him, doubtless because of their provenance in more glorious times. They strolled about; sat; had a Polish lunch – cabbage, potatoes, croquettes – which for two came to the same price as his American breakfast for one. He ate as if he hadn't for months. It was a way she could please him, she saw. And to please him, she realized now in some shock, was a thing she longed to do.

Pale golden light shone through dissipating greys. Pre-evening colours gilded the steep roofs and gabled windows of the houses around the square, reminding her of Siena. It was the same aura, late medieval, as if arrested in time. But Siena had been with Leoline, before she'd discovered his first betrayal; and the memory evoked only pain. Besides, everything there had been authentic, whereas this was all reconstructed.

'Isn't the real Poland,' Krzysztof was forced to confess.

'Don't crush my illusions, at least not today.'

She stopped to buy postcards. A Polish woman before her paid 3,000 zł. for five. Then came her turn and she held out five cards as well, but the middle-aged hippy peddlar demanded 5,000 from her through brown teeth.

She glanced to Krzysztof. He said something sharp.

'Never mind,' she declared, having got a signal she wanted. 'What's two thousand złotys? ten pence? No need to be a hero over that.'

A drizzle succeeded the brief rush of gold in the sky, driving them back to the centre. Stopping in front of the Warsaw *Nike* statue, they studied its straining, arching, half-naked form with sword in hand glowering towards a West out of which *Blitzkrieg* had raged. Geraldine thought it fine: as fine in its way as the 'Balzac' of Rodin, which Lord Clark of Civilization had identified as an apogee of Romantic art. But whereas 'Balzac''s attraction had been in its evocation of maleness – not the trivial willies in graffiti consciousness so much as a titanic father-godliness – *Nike* was both bisexual and transcendent of sex altogether: a great phallic shape joined to breasts like a Valkyrie's armour and hair streaming back as if one of Shelley's maenads on the storm.

'Magnificent!' our lady lecturer murmured. 'A grand poem to Energy!' – And she was pleased to be able to voice this without being twitted for pretention as might have been back in London.

A harder rain forced them on across the great square and into the shelter of the War Memorial. And here Krzysztof lingered, as if to demand of her that she look as long at it as at the *Nike*. So Geraldine studied the eternal flame and the flowers; the brace of sentinel soldiers shivering in parade dress; the names of battles fought in the Middle Ages to create for the Jagiellons the most far-flung empire in Europe since Rome, or in the struggle against 'Fascism and Hiterlism' from the swift engorgement of the nation in 1939 through the heroic fight of Polish troops with the Allies at Monte Cassino, or in the pyrrhic victory by the side of the Red Army in the last days of the War.

Gazing, her mind strayed. More and more it was starting to focus on the moment of decision arriving. They had passed many hotels; no word had been spoken. Krzysztof's car was at the Marriott, so they had to go back there. But what then?

He led her on through a park towards the spire of the Palace of Kultur. Statues of women, some nude, others in 17th century finery eroded, marked the paths here. They brought to mind the Luxembourg Gardens: another city-scape full of Leoline, thus pain. Like the buds on the branches, these counterparts of French queens took a harsh punishment from the cold, steady drizzle. Children marched out by their grannies for afternoon air were marched in again. And Geraldine's consciousness drifted with them from the statues towards something she'd been longing for more and more recently, until the implications became almost apparent.

'Brrr!' – She squeezed his arm again. 'You know what I'd fancy right now? A sauna or solarium or something like that; some sensual pleasure, wouldn't you?'

He glanced at her as if she'd proposed they swing naked from the Marriott's chandeliers.

'Don't worry!' she laughed. 'A cappuccino will do.'

So they returned to neo-Vienna, where the shy girl from Łódź had played violin. – She was there still, though no longer wearing the homely dress her mother had sewn. Done up in silver *lamé* like her cohorts, she had traded in Mozart for a Broadway tune.

'All ends as it began, in the American Palace of Culture,' Geraldine mused.

'Our new Poland!' Krzysztof forbore to reply, a transformation as quick as a magister student who becomes a call-girl at night after being a lustreless lecturee by day.

Around the *rez-de-chaussée*, lower middle-class locals spent their week's wages on cake and a dream. From a table nearby, a burly West German pimp ran tarted-up Russiennes for the needs of visiting 'biznezmen'. In the spirit of this, a transient *roué* murmured 'Hello?' to Geraldine in passing.

'Move on!' Krzysztof demanded, his cheekbones standing out, making him look really Slavic for the first time. – With nostrils flared, he recalled a medallion of a Renaissance condottiere Leo had bought her in Siena, Geraldine mused.

Saying 'Sorry!', the *roué* retreated. And Krzysztof sat back down tremblingly, his face red round the ears yet utterly white, as if asphyxiated, in the middle.

His breathing was laboured. And with a suddenness that shocked her, Geraldine wanted to feel him. She wanted to have him then and there.

'I think you're lovely,' she managed.

The river was crossed.

✳

They sat in the breakfast room of the Polonia Hotel. There was a German couple at one of the three other tables, no one else. The waitress came in with coffee and rolls: it was 6:30 a.m.: she looked surly. Neither Geraldine nor Krzysztof spoke.

Geraldine was scheduled to fly back to London at 8:30. Krzysztof thought she looked half-departed already as she gazed at a large, blue-green oil-painting above the Germans' table. There were many like it in old Party hotels in Poland, but this was more splendid than most. In the midst of its huge space and dark hues sat a blonde woman, static and statuesque; behind her as far as the eye could see spread steppes of the Eurasian plain and onion-domes of Orthodox churches. The scene gave off a solidity and power like that which had attracted Geraldine to the *Nike*; and Krzysztof wondered if, from images like it, she might be half able to fall in love with his country.

'I'd like to buy that,' she mused. 'Reminds me of Mme Hańska.'

'Please?'

'The Ukrainian aristocrat Balzac married before he died. He exhausted himself writing 100 books in 20 years. Hurtling back and forth across Europe to see her finished him off. But then love is built on enthusiasm, not self-protection.'

She sipped at muddy coffee. Her eyes showed how little sleep she had had. Krzysztof felt guilty about eating her food and staying in this expensive (for a Pole) hotel. Maybe he'd paid his share by performing as she'd wanted; but then he'd slept like a boy being watched over by mummy, and that made him feel ignominious.

Her eyes were glassed-over. They seemed to swim in a myriad of vague possibilities that had little to do with her life as she'd lived it till now. This alarmed him. Agnieszka and the other Polish girls he had known were romantic when called for but never lost sight of practical considerations such as babies and jobs. That's why he had always played the artful dodger with them. With Geraldine by contrast, he was out of his depth.

What had she been after? just one night? Should he make a show of wanting to see her again? 'Would you hurtle back and forth across Europe to see someone, like Balzac?' he asked.

Her gaze remained stuck to the painting. Shouldn't have said that; came out sounding too clever. Besides, he was no male equivalent of a Ukrainian countess, was he? Why would a woman like this want to hurtle back and forth across Europe to see him?

'I think it might finish me off too,' she mused. 'But who knows? Maybe she should have travelled to Paris to see *him*.'

Was this an invitation to London? Could the liaison become the potential Big Chance for a poor Polish lad?

'On the other hand,' she sighed, as if mesmerized by the image, which Krzysztof now thought looked a little like her, 'how could you persuade an iconness like that to budge?'

He delivered her to the airport, then came back to the hotel. 'Here,' she had said, handing him a credit for another breakfast which she'd fished out of her bag while searching for passport;

'take this and eat a second breakfast on me – you have such a healthy appetite. And after last night, you need to restore your strength.'

He felt drained, it was true. So he went back the little breakfast room and surly waitress and sat over a second boiled egg and gazed at the painting.

Actually, now that he was back on his own, Krzysztof felt more than just drained. A bundle of twitches and strange effects made it seem as if *he* were the Westerner just arrived in Poland. Lighting a cigarette, he sipped more muddy coffee, knowing he shouldn't do either: Polish cigarettes were a reason life expectancy for males here was ten years lower than in the West, and coffee aged you twice as fast as tea.

So Agnieszka never tired of telling him. She was always nagging about such things, Agnieszka… Hadn't thought about her for nearly a week: not since they'd pinned up those posters for Geraldine's readings. 'Why have they chosen you to drive her?' she'd asked. 'Is it because you're better looking than Marek or Tomaś? I think it's disgusting. When a man comes, they assign him the prettiest girl; now for a woman it's the prettiest boy. You'd think our country was a brothel!'

Krzysztof had smiled. He'd always loved it the way she got cross. She was always so clear about what she wanted and so calculating in her little fits to get it; it made him feel manly. That was one reason she made a show of resisting whenever he tried to get amorous with her. But Agnieszka's resistance was two-thirds calculation: really she loved it when he broke through. She'd even loved it the time she'd made him so furious that he'd slapped her on the bottom and left an imprint for a week.

'Look what you've done!' she'd protested the next time he'd seen her and raised her skirt and pulled down her *majtiki* to display the brand. – She'd done this with a scowl on her slightly Kirghizian features. But he had known she'd been pleased really, because it had meant that she belonged to him.

For his part it had excited him so much that he had almost had an accident in his trousers and grabbed her hand so she could take responsibility for it. And now he grew hard again thinking about it. But of course Agnieszka had rarely let him go all the way. A good Polish Catholic despite her father's Tartar blood, she had determined not to use birth control or risk abortion. For the longest time she hadn't let him have her at all: the sort of behaviour that had caused the slap. Then she'd consented and, consulting her thermometer, scheduled the loss of her virginity down to the moment of least risk. Maybe because this was also the moment of most pre-menstrual tension, it had turned out acrimonious, as well as frustratingly brief. Virginity is a nuisance, Krzysztof had concluded, adding himself to a standard typology of Polish male.

To tell the truth, waiting for the few chances before Agnieszka's period had become annoying in the extreme. This was one of the reasons why his night with Geraldine had been such a revelation. *She* had had none of his little girl's inhibitions. If there had been a factor of control, it had been the reverse. Instead of an incessant squeezing together of legs, resulting in efforts to pry them apart, the lady professor had laid herself open. More had been her hunger, not less; and Krzysztof had found it almost too much the way she had moaned, 'Don't stop! keep going!', as if each time he had finished, she'd wished he'd only just begun.

'Do you want more?' he'd asked, panting, expecting a satisfied 'No'. But fondling his genitals, the English lady had murmured:

'Don't be silly. Of course!'

He went back in the room now – still only 9:30 – grey day over Warsaw. The key didn't have to be returned till noon, so he lay down on her one of the two pushed-together beds.

The pillow smelled of her – face powder or something – and he grew confused. What had happened to him? Agnieszka would be in a fury: 'Is that all you think of yourself? just some pretty boy to be used by any middle-aged Western woman who comes here? The next thing you'll be going with men!' – She would be right. How could he have let it happen? And what was the matter with these Western women that they should have behaved as Geraldine had? Were the stories old Party-members used to tell true? Were all Westerners just immoral decadents?

He felt tight in the chest. 'Where does it hurt?' his sweet imp

21

might have asked, like Zerlina in the performance of *Don Giovanni* which they'd gone to see the previous week. But Zerlina was not here now, and this Masetto could not go to her; she would know in an instant that something had happened, like Masetto after Zerlina had slipped off with the Don. My God, life is an effort, Krzysztof thought. And if I feel like this at twenty-two, what on earth am I going to feel like at thirty, let alone her age – thirty-five. Or was it forty?

Thoughts of Geraldine's age made him want to run back to Agnieszka and stay with her for the rest of his life; stay in Poland, take that job down in Łódź that he'd heard at the conference might be going. He was almost finished his thesis; he had experience of universities in the West, so he had a chance, didn't he? – He would apply. Yes, that would be the right thing: get a good job, in Poland. He could see visiting Westerners from time to time, and from time to time he could put up with the strain of being charming for them. As long as it was from time to time and no more, it might even be 'fun' – that word she'd kept using, whatever it meant... Seemed like tension to him, like a high wire act.

He dozed.

The door opened and in she stepped. And Krzysztof was shocked as well as excited to see her take off her clothes and, without explanation, take his off too. Nor could he do now the slightest thing to stop her from performing exactly as she pleased.

Did she have control over what seemed to him like near madness? He had to assume so. Because shortly his mind had shut down, as it were. All his intelligence, all his consciousness seemed to be being drawn from his brain into the strainings of what she called his 'lovely willy'. She would think for them both now, this seemed to say. – It made him feel a strange relief.

Krzysztof had never taken a drug. He had never even got drunk on the vodka his father used to: his mother's misery had inured him to that. But in this state he was entering, he felt like that must have: like the junkies who roved glaze-eyed down Krakówskie Przedmieście, or drunks who did loop-de-loops along Marszałkowska Street after the off-licenses had opened.

This sex with her: there had never been anything like it in his experience, and it scared him. He could feel his heart labouring and imagined his own death. And who would have believed it, that you could sense your own death for the first time in an act of sex? Or was it of love? No, couldn't have been. Still, she was moaning, as if death were in it for her too: as if the act were somehow absolutely essential to keep her going.

Did she do it out of fear then? If so, fear of what?

'I lost my pearls,' she announced after the second or third bout. 'They're worth £1,000, which is five times the cost of a plane ticket. It seemed well worth it to come back.'

Was she embarrassed? Given her entrance, it seemed obvious that she hadn't come back for pearls. As they lay there hot and heavy-breathing, did she feel a need for a fig-leaf?

'Have you seen them?' she asked, getting up and crossing the sex-scented room.

He eyed her as she ransacked drawers and overturned cushions. Her skin was white, but not the blue-white of Agnieszka's. She seemed faintly freckled, as if her hair were red, though on top it was blonde and in the pubic area dark. Her breasts had wide nipples, much larger than his girl's: they were large altogether, the largest he'd known, and quite attractive in shape – a kind you wanted to hide your head between or suck mindlessly. Her waist was quite shapely, given the size of her hips; the thighs below it belonged to what a peasant might call a *real* woman. Could he satisfy her, was the question this raised.

Disconsolate, she continued casting about. 'Was the room made by the time you got back?'

'I guess.'

'Then the maid's been here, and it's useless.'

'Please?'

'She's stolen them. They're gone.'

Was she upset really? Was this pearl story true? He hadn't noticed them on her. Well maybe, on that last night in Kraków as she'd laughed with Twitch: laughed and flirted with the famous English professor while hardly acknowledging his presence where he'd sat among the younger Polish colleagues. And wasn't that how it would be with her always? near denial of his existence in public and exploitative passion otherwise?

'You couldn't be a darling and go to the desk and ask them?'

'Please?'

'If they've found my pearls. Your brains aren't all down in that thing, are they?'

The 'thing', now shrivelled, was in full retreat. And Krzysztof leapt off the bed wondering what she thought of men really.

Pulling his pants up, he asked himself: is she one of these women you hear about who think men are good for nothing but money or sex? Surlily, he started out.

'I'm sorry,' she breathed, catching him from behind. 'I don't mean to be ratty.' – He could feel those great breasts spreading soft round his backbone. 'It's not only their cost; it's their sentimental value. Somebody gave them to me a long time ago, someone gone from my life now. They're all I have to remember it by.'

She was good at this, he thought going down in the lift: so good that he would become her knight errant and do whatsoever she pleased. Which thought was followed by a twinge of shame, mixed with pain for Agnieszka. But what other choice did he have than to drive her and show her the best of Poland? If she wanted charm, he was obliged to give it. If she wanted sex, he was obliged to give that too, no? Poland was Western, part of the club now. He had simply to accept his fate, like everyone else.

This was one part of what Krzysztof was thinking. Another was made up of genuine curiosity and attraction to her.

'They have not seen them,' he said, coming back to the room. 'But I asked about the painting.'

She was sitting on a chair beyond the thin curtains, staring at the Palace of Kultur, hands between thighs.

'Painting?' she murmured.

'The one in the breakfast room. Of the Slavic woman. The one you so liked.'

'Ah. But no pearls. The swine.'

'Please?'

'Never mind. Serves me right. What on earth was I thinking, bringing a thing of such value to a place like this?'

He hesitated. 'Not for sale, they said.'

'What isn't?'

'The painting.'

She took her hands from where they were resting and raised them towards him. 'You sweet boy! You don't mean to say you wanted to *buy* it for me? But you couldn't afford that. Come here, beautiful thing!'

What was he to her: a child or a man?

'They said we could try on Krakówskie Przedmieście.'

'Try what, my beauty?' – She plucked at his shirt.

'One of the galleries. They might have one like it.'

'One what?' – She was sex-drunk evidently: one of those women the Americans called (he had trouble with the word) a nymphomaniac?

'A painting.'

'O darling, forget about paintings; it's you I want. Get those clothes off!'

'But, don't you think it's getting a bit late?'

'Late for what?'

'To get the key back.'

'We'll stay on here; where else is there to go? You told me yourself you live with your mother: all Poles do till your age, unless they're married. Which reminds me: why aren't you married? Aren't gay, are you? a pretty boy like you?'

Krzysztof shot up like a soldier. It made her giggle.

'What are you laughing about?'

'I'm sorry. It's a compliment really. I've almost never laid eyes on a man as pretty as you. And in England when a man is very beautiful, he's almost always assumed to be that way.'

'Well not in Poland. Not always.'

'Of course not. But if you're not going to come over here and kiss me, then what are we going to do?'

He pondered a moment. 'The British Airways flight goes in the afternoon. You could still make that.'

Now her smile faded. 'You're not happy I'm back?'

'Of course I'm happy – was happy. But don't you need to get home?'

'Not really.'

'You mean you want to *stay* here?' – He didn't intend to make it sound strained with disbelief, but it did.

'Is Poland *that* bad?'

'Not for a Pole, but...' He felt abashed now: ashamed again, though differently.

'One of the professors at Łódź – is that how you pronounce it? – asked me if I wanted to give a lecture there. I thought maybe, if you didn't have to get back to your classes, you could drive me. I'd pay, of course.'

'To Łódź?'

'Ah, that's how you pronounce it. Yes. Is it far?'

Krzysztof explained that it was quite close, quite convenient. As he did, an idea came to him, quite alien, exploitative. But this was what Western life was about, wasn't it? using influence? getting the upper hand? To go down to Łódź and be seen as her friend might impress the old ladies who ran the Institute there. And impressing them might be a way to land that job that was going. And so, ironically, through this erotic madness with her, he might get Agnieszka and marriage and babies and the normal life the respectable part of him craved.

✳

Geraldine herself was swimming. It had been years since she'd let down her discipline to this extent – not since Leoline, in Siena, just before she'd discovered that, while she'd been burning the midnight oil on her first book, he'd been fondling one of the tenants in one of his shopping-malls in Southwark in lieu of payment of rent. In fact, on the road on this spring afternoon in Poland, as the dull weather lifted, there came a light she recalled – Continental, rich with indistinct memories and future promise. It looked Mediterranean even as the sun lowered, shadows crossed the fields and farmers led their workhorses back to their tethering-spots for the night.

As they came into town, sunset shone dead ahead, casting its long, red-orange streaks through a haze. Pollution in brown gauze covered the place, like the red glow of London at night, which she used to gaze at from Leoline's bedroom above

Cantelowes Square. Chimneys of textile and chemical plants, the ones not yet closed down, sent plumes into the deepening indigo, tinging it ochre.

'Łódź is one of the most polluted cities in Poland,' Krzysztof observed. And Poland is one of the most polluted countries in the world, she forbore to reply.

'But it makes sunset dramatic, doesn't it?' she said as they came into the main street.

Łódź was the second city of Poland in size, he went on, though not quite in elegance. The street was filled with *art nouveau* palaces built by German and Jewish merchant-princes in the late 19th century: immigrants who had made it a great industrial centre for this part of the world. Both were gone now, the Jews eliminated by the Nazis (Łódź had been the last outpost of the Reich), the Germans by the Red Army, both with help from the Poles. The 40% of the population which had been Jewish had been replaced by Poles driven out of the Eastern territories which Churchill and Roosevelt had ceded to Stalin. As a result, few on the street felt historical attachment to place. Partly because of that, the buildings were falling to bits even more than their counterparts up in Warsaw. And here buildings were original, not facsimiles rebuilt by UNESCO and Communist bureaucrats after the War.

Łódź, in short, was one of those sad corners of Earth which had the ironic misfortune of never having been flattened.

'Not with a bang but a whimper,' Geraldine breathed.

'Please?'

'It's pathetic!' she marvelled.

'What?'

'It's so beautiful, and *so* decayed. It could be the Milan of the north, if anyone cared.'

'You mean, if anyone had the money.'

She observed, fascinated, while he parked beside a grey stucco structure named, or misnamed, Grand Hotel. They could contact the university people later, she decided, not wishing her liaison to be limited too soon by the scrutiny of local hosts. Nor did she want the lively impressions now flowing to be adulterated by some party-line, pre- or post-Communist.

27

While he went in to see about a room, she lingered in the gloaming and watched the light fade over crumbling pediments. Lamps came on, feeble compared to London or New York, or even Vicksburg, Mississippi. The place seemed a dead city: Łódź *la morte*, she nick-named it, recycling Rodenbach.

Ambling a few steps along from the Grand, she came upon a plaque: the birthplace of Artur Rubenstein. And Jerzy Kościński had been born here too, she recalled: a host of cultivated Jews who had fled, first from Russia and pogroms, then from their 'promised land' and the camps to Zion or dreams of the West... An eerie halo stretched over the scene: a strange, almost palpable fabric, as of spirits floating half-dead, unappeased. It was, spooky, other-worldly yet quite moving all at once.

'Flaubert preferred tinsel to silver,' she remarked to Krzysztof when he re-emerged.

'Please?' – He took her arm to lead her into the lobby.

'He preferred tinsel to silver because it had pathos. Do you understand?' she asked, stopping him short of the desk.

Thick middle-aged men in uniforms loitered about, ready to lift bags or bounce anyone who came in drunk or disorderly. An aura of unreconstructed Tsarist or Stalinist authoritarianism hung around: heavy, torpid, complacent. Through glass doors to a café, Geraldine spied a rotund woman in furs shovelling down a cream tart. It was as if winter had not left here and Communism never ended: as if time had wound down and, like Balaam's ass, simply refused to go on.

A great spreading inertia seemed to pervade, in the midst of which waited this beautiful boy, gazing at her. And what would happen to him in time, she wondered. Would the Chopin-like cheekbones be hidden by pockets of flesh? Would the lean bones become a hanging-place for thirty years of foul diet? Would his colour turn liverish from slow asphyxiation? – Even in off the street, the noisome air continued to taste of fumes.

'Łódź *la morte*,' she repeated.

He frowned, as if worried for her state of mind.

'Sorry,' she giggled and, slipping a hand back through his arm: 'Do they have a room, darling? And make sure it has a bath, will you please?'

The smell was musty, but through cheap lacy curtains there was a view of the street. Down the corridor was a bar; on its door she had read, 'Hotel patrons only'. In and out had strolled women, garish with cosmetics, tawdry by London standards, more like from somewhere in the depressed north of Britain.

Geraldine felt quite different from how she had up in Warsaw. In Warsaw she had been cossetted, with the Marriott Hotel close at hand and the airport; if anything had gone wrong, there was the embassy or Man from the World Bank. In Warsaw she'd been someone: her Western credentials had mattered, and what she had done with a boy may have been arbitrary and unrepeatable, but it was her own choice that governed. In Warsaw she'd been able to feel relatively clean and sure. But here?

Degeneration seemed to seep around her like a leak in the gas. She had a glimpse of chaos out of Dostoyevsky and wondered if, half-imperceptibly, she might begin to slip down into some abyss. Sex with Krzysztof had begun as a lark, as therapy in her view, as an oasis of youth and calm on the road back from Kraków. It had been so pastoral and he so reassuring; besides, she'd felt so desperate. Why? And what else could she have done? turned back to Leoline Hooper?

She'd considered that once or twice – even tried it on occasion, letting him back into her bed, only to close her legs. Leo's betrayals had been frankly too awful, though she had to accept now that she'd been partly to blame. He had wanted her back and was tortured by it, she knew and privately took comfort from this – even in subtle ways worked to maintain it. This was wicked, she knew but justified herself by saying that Leo was an adult, that in matters of love anything goes and that he had betrayed her just one too many times.

Still, she ought to have let him off the hook – ought to have pushed him to marry one of those floozies he had had in the years since she'd moved out of Cantelowes Square. But she hadn't. Nor, despite offers, had she taken anyone into the flat she'd moved into in Highbury Fields. Old men like Twitch and mere boys like the Sri Lankan student who'd become a world-famous novelist – she'd not let one of them in. And now in her forties what had seemed like a sensible way to proceed was beginning to strike her as the prelude to a life of what used to be called an old maid.

She had seen this spectre glowering at her for years. She taught Eng lit, after all: hadn't the type had been one of its staples since at least the days of Jane Austen? In her twenties Geraldine had lived through a 'revolution': a wall had come down; women had flocked through to build new lives, as mannish girls, as traditional women, as various types in between. Anything had gone then; still, women had remained women; and whatever New Age benefits had accrued, there were still age-old conflicts – between duty and desire, the demands of the world and self-realization, family and profession *et cetera*. Women remained human and so were still racked – about loneliness: how to combat or cope with it? and purpose: what was the great effort about finally? Was it about accomplishment: more academic distinctions, books published, shopping-malls built, as for Leoline? Was it about pleasure? spring idylls, new lovers or part-ners pulled? Or was it, at last, about reproducing the species?

Under her mask, Geraldine had come to believe in this as a primary truth. Yet to arrive at such a conclusion was not the same as to discover any easy way forward. What did it mean to admit to oneself that one wanted a child? only to be in a position that women of no sophistication had been in since the beginning of time: how to conceive, when and with whom. Of course her situation had been different: most women were hunters for more than just sperm and genes; they needed a man for support – she did not. She had her career and her salary: a man's presence would intrude. A man's control, which is what normally came with his aid, would be frankly unwelcome, wouldn't it?

So she had thought, or rationalized. And in fact, she had thought more about this subject than anyone knew, though most of her thoughts had been semi-conscious, or at best half-thought out, by the time she'd met Krzysztof Robiński and 'chemistry' (as that's how she characterized it) had ensued. But in this depressed town where the real difference in their worlds could not be disguised, she was starting to wake up. – She'd been running wild. Why? She'd been doing it at least in part to give a jolt to her system. She had dreamt of conceiving: attraction to him had been a symptom and prelude to that. But did she *really* want to do so now, and in such a bizarre, shabby setting, and with someone as unsuitable as this poor Polish lad, beautiful though to her he had seemed?

They went to the café for a drink before dinner. It was the nearest one could get to luxury in Łódź. Like the Polonia in Warsaw, the Grand was standard old system: decayed 1950s, again like in some moribund town in the north of England. There were linen cloths on round, formica-topped tables surrounded by aluminium swivel chairs with low backs and fake-leather seats. In one corner, a piano tinkled 'I'm in the Mood for Love'; the door to the street banged; through plate-glass windows, Geraldine could see several thick taxi-drivers in leather jackets having an argument under a street-lamp. It looked like it might end in fists.

'I'm in the mood for love'? No, it was hardly romantic here. The pervasive torpor made it seem as if she might gradually lose spark and slide into sitting at one of these tables forever. The weight of her hips and lower half of her body seemed to sink and spread over the seat. Slow-motioned, beyond sex or perhaps even desire, could she become one of these women, eternally sipping coffee and chewing cake with bovine deliberation. Some sought to appear elegant, adjusting scarves round their necks; and after a fashion, it worked. But all had the wide faces of the great Slavic plain: no sharpness nor animation except in the case of one or two young molls who sat next to more brick-built, leather-jacketed types.

The piano moved on to 'Red Roses for a Blue Lady': more apt in title, at least the second part. The taxi-drivers stopped their ruckus in the street and were embracing and kissing in a kind of dance… Geraldine looked to Krzysztof. What was he thinking, this child-man of hers? that she was a monster who had just used him as she pleased? Not yet, surely. Reaching a hand out, she touched his fingertips. The nails were clean, small. All of them had small hands: small for their sizes, even the thick-set drivers, unlike Englishmen like Leoline, whose hands had often seemed too big to her. But this hand retracted. Why? Wasn't it on to show affection in public here?

Raising the hand, he motioned to a sour-faced waitress with no neck and uniform smelling of hours of work. Ambling over, she presented Geraldine with a bill. Krzysztof intercepted it, looked and, calling her back, had a few words. 'Has she put too much on?' Geraldine asked; 'never mind.' But his blood was up as with the postcard-seller in Warsaw; and before she could add that nothing had to be proved here, she realized that it was not for her that he was arguing. 'Don't make a scene – it's hardly worth it.' But he was demanding the manager; the waitress obliged; and soon an unholy row had ensued.

The manager was another brick-built type with cantilevered neck who looked as if he would have had Krzysztof beaten up in the street as soon as listen to his complaint. Still the boy argued. They had over-charged by 100%, he averred. The waitress and manager both justified the amount by some small print on the menu, to which they pointed. To Geraldine it meant nothing, less than fifty pence, but to Krzysztof:

'I have told them we will not pay!' – The manager stalked off; other customers gawped. 'He says we must, or he will call the police. I told him to do his worst!'

This sounded like a prelude to disaster. And our lady needed all her diplomatic skills to persuade the manager – to say nothing of the police, who did arrive – not to worry, she would pay. But that was not before the boy had been held down in his seat by five Lech Wałęsa-mustachioed types in uniform and a Polish-American onlooker, interpreting for her, warned:

'You must pay really; it's better. They mean business here. Communism may be dead in the headlines, but with little officials like this nothing has changed.'

She got him out of there, thinking, 'Food, that's the solution!' She took them to the restaurant, a large, high-ceilinged chamber with puttis and cornucopias on the upper walls, painted gold. Here too a memory of elegance floated in tandem with more vulgarity of a tired, '50s-style present: a small parquet dance-floor occupied half of the space, a mirrored globe dangling above it. A band played lugubrious rock-and-roll while a middle-aged man swirled in a ghost of a foxtrot with a teenaged girl, presumably his daughter.

Their party looked on from a table nearby.

'Name day,' Krzysztof murmured.

'Sorry?'

'It is her name day, the girl's: the feast day of the saint she's named after. The family has come from their village, Zduńska Wola or some such, to celebrate.'

'Ah.'

Pathos again.

Only one other table was occupied. At it sat what appeared to be a pimp and a whore, drinking Russian champagne. Krzysztof and Geraldine were placed next to them and given huge menus. 'Heartbreak Hotel' crooned as she ordered Weinerschnitzel, imagining it the least dicey.

Krzysztof chose wild boar. Many of them still existed in the forests around Łódź and up by Białystok, he explained: the 'virgin forests' which, according to local belief, had never been cut down or replanted.

'I wonder what will happen once the American and Japanese multinationals move in,' she mused.

It was back to this now, talk about issues of the day, as if from two journalists over a beer. Geraldine said no to wine, fearing it might make him unpredictable again. However, between courses, she did consent to a dance. And it did feel rather sweet trying to recall how to foxtrot to a Slavic version of 'Love Me Tender'. Krzysztof danced quite correctly, like a cadet or a schoolboy. They had another turn after dessert, and she found herself wishing she could pass him on to the girl whose name day it was. But it was too late now; the river had been crossed. Time for bed again, and what could she do?

'I'm knackered!' she exclaimed on the stairs as he kissed her.

His face seemed to darken, making him very handsome again. And it occurred to her then that a real danger zone might be being reached: that under the force of her amorous binge, he might be falling in love. If so, what folly! because she felt nothing for him now; only pity, and affection. It had been a fling and was over. He'd slipped out of her heart in the café below; she felt the space he had left, but he was gone, just like that, and she closed.

What to pretend? headache? her period coming on?

In the room, she undressed with blithe lack of ceremony and slipped on her nightgown without bothering to wash. Bustling into her one of the forlorn single beds, she watched him stare at the floor like a disconsolate child.

'I'm sorry,' she murmured. 'I am *so* tired.'

He tapped out a cigarette, lit it.

She had to be good now. She'd been bad, exploitative, perhaps evil in effect; but there was nothing to do but get beyond it – go give the lecture she'd been invited to give, do the requisite dinner with local academe, then up to Warsaw and plane for home.

As for him? – She longed to tell him it had just been a lark. But as he stood there dejected, she felt sure it wouldn't do. There was the language gap, culture, age. And what if his temper flared up again and he stormed off, leaving her in this dead place at the end of the world, with its unreconstructed Communists?

Intimations of that drove Geraldine down down, into an unfamiliar slough of despond – a kind of brown-black sludge out of which she had to pull herself with deliberation, thinking, 'This is ridiculous. One has to take responsibility for what one has done. One must end as one began: follow through!' So she got out of bed and, going over to him, purred:

'There, there, my lovely. Don't just stand like this looking so glum. I'm a little tired of life at the minute, that's all. It has nothing whatsoever to do with you.'

✳

Krzysztof was missing the music. Birds were here too, despite the pollution; they were audible amid the soughings of young leaves. Out on the streets there were interesting moments: spring brought romanticism out of the Polish soul. The evening before as they'd come into town, he'd seen a young couple half-dancing against sunset along Narutowicza Street. Then at a tram-stop by the Opera Square, a woman's hand had reached out of a carriage to make funny shapes of her boyfriend's nose as he stood by the window saying goodbye to her. What did the West have better than this? telephones that worked? – Geraldine had spent half the night trying to get through to her hosts and to London. The latter had not succeeded; the former had. So now she was going to a lecture and lunch with the director of the local philological institute. – Krzysztof had not been invited.

'What shall I do?' he asked.

'Whatever you want to,' she stated. 'Go to the Park; it's a lovely day. Go back to Warsaw if you have to; I could always get up there by train.'

A look on his face must have betrayed his reaction.

'O don't pull a moody! just go and have fun. And no arguments in cafés either: you don't need to defend my honour today. You've proved you're a man by a far more satisfactory method.'

She almost winked then. Rushing out, she added:

'Don't bother to get up. It's probably better for both of us if we're not seen together too much.'

So much for his fantasy of a foot in the door, fine job and marriage. And what a rage it put him into! Here he had been fucking himself silly – for what? not for love, nor advancement nor even money. The lady had given him nothing, though the job he'd performed had gone much further than agreed to up in Warsaw. He'd spent a fortune in petrol, and if he didn't have his valves fixed in a hundred kilometres or so, the Polski Fiat would surely break down.

He wanted to call Agnieszka. He wished her sweet little body were there beside his. He would have a lot of new things to teach it, but knew he couldn't – not all at once. He'd have to slip in each technique one by one as born out of spontaneous desire… The animal tenderness with which he would chase and bind his little sprite – he grew hard again thinking about it. He could feel himself sneaking up on her like some great cat and biting her neck… But this wouldn't do. He threw off the covers and smacked his erection. What if *she* came back and wanted it 'again and again' like before and he couldn't perform? That would truly be an end to his purpose and humiliating coda to their wild ride.

Crossly, he dressed and went down for breakfast.

He had the two credits that came with the room (Geraldine had rushed off too fast to use hers), but the hotel café was out.

The thick-necked drivers stared at him as he stepped into the street. A sharp mix of fear and scorn drilled into the back of his neck: word had got round – gigolo to the rich English lady. Still, the sun on Piotrkówska was almost majestic. In the brilliance of morning, it *did* almost look like a 'Milan of the North', as she'd said. Not that Krzysztof had ever been to the one in the south, nor many fine, sunlit places for that matter.

Some developer should come here, he thought, ambling forth: patch up the buildings, fix the holes in the tarmac – better still, turn the whole place into a shopping precinct like they had in Pittsburgh. And what it would look like then? Pictures of Copenhagen rose to his mind, or the Rynek in Kraków. And people would come here to behave well then, not to have sordid, exploitative affairs in corrupt old Communist hot-beds like the Grand. They would linger in front of Secessionist palaces turned into elegant bars and shops. Polish people would be prosperous then, not down to their last 100,000 złotys, like him...

At the state-run café, tables with umbrellas were set out on the porch. Customers took coffee and ice cream in the sun. The sun was expensive. So rare was it here that it might have been valued at the price of a ticket to Spain. Krzysztof would have liked to have taken off his clothes and sprawled in it, and the idea gave a rise in his trousers again. Why was it that sex just made you want more sex? After four times in the night and God knows how many the day before, how could his body still be reacting like this?

Three girls were sitting at one of the other tables: pretty, pale-skinned blondes like Agnieszka. Now and then one of them would look at him and giggle, which wound him up more. The waitress who brought coffee smiled. Now why did she do that? Waitresses in darkest Poland didn't smile: not slim, pretty ones like this. Was he giving off some scent? Could they see through his trousers? What would Agnieszka say? that he was turning into a sex-object all of a sudden? that job, marriage and babies would not be the fate of a James Dean?

He slipped on dark-glasses and, taking out his notebook, began to sketch. He did not sketch the waitress, nor the three girls primping, but a woman under an umbrella further away who sat reading a book. Wavy brown hair fell to her shoulders; a wide-collared jacket, open at the neck, exposed the cavity between her shoulder-blades, though not so much as to hint at cleavage. Something clean and virtuous hovered about her, at the same time quite sensual. A small crucifix gleamed on the bit of skin disappearing into her blouse – oddly reassuring. Krzysztof even admired the thick, wire-rimmed glasses that obscured her eyes, suggesting that he could draw her for as long as he liked without her noticing and thinking he was trying to pick her up.

The waitress and three girls lost interest in him when they saw his attention gone elsewhere. Absorbed in his task, he thought: I should do this more often; it makes the world calm, you lose track of time and come back to yourself. The sensuality was quite different from what he had experienced with Geraldine. That had been all appetite, physical, material; this was all beatitude, like some prelude of Chopin after a bombastic rhapsody by Liszt. This was like pale sun through leaves on a halcyon spring morning: innocent, tender, replenishing hope. And by the time he had finished, Krzysztof was ready to saunter down Piotrkówska in a vague musical nimbus, deciding not to fix his car or even bother to use it but, following Geraldine's suggestion, to spend the rest of the day in a park drawing the trees and the grasses or just discarding his clothes and lolling in a rye-field listening to bird song to his heart's content.

He stood at the corner of Piotrkówska and Zielona awaiting a tram. The sun had risen to direct overhead; it cascaded down a peeled stucco wall behind him, pouring its unusual gold on his skull. Arched slightly forward, he loitered as if stupid with languor and heat.

A crowd had formed at the stop, men in shirt-sleeves and sandals, women in thin cotton dresses, except for the old. The old shuffled past encased in the same heavy coats they wore day-in and day-out regardless of weather. Fuzzy, threadbare, impregnated with sweat and fine dust, these seemed to have grown into their owners' skins and become inseparable from them. Brown and grey, the native colours of place, they exuded a torpor that seemed to him almost subhuman.

A lifetime of subjection to Browns of the West or Reds of the East had taught them to be martyrs or just to give up. My sad country! he thought. But was it his? Krzysztof felt no identity with these ancient, sad creatures; only sorrow for them and repugnance. Like many of his generation in the 'new' East, he believed he would never fall into their condition. The political context was different now, wasn't it? no longer brown or red, but rainbow-coloured.

He had dressed this morning in a standard new Eastern costume of tight-fitting t-shirt, designer training-shoes and baggy, ersatz-silken track pants. Geraldine had scoffed at this version of a perceived Western style, and with her he'd kept on the coat and tie the Institute had encouraged him to wear. But that was the *real* costume – pre-1989, nomenklatura Poland – and since she'd gone off without him today, he had determined to wear exactly what he liked!

Had he been in the West, he might have been listening to earphones, separating himself further from mastodons of the past. In the East a mere student could not yet afford what was standard fare for his ex-classmates at Pittsburgh. Still, the mere thought of that freedom and Americanish style set a rock-tune winding through his heat-sodden brain, pulsing to the tick of his blood as he leant there James Dean-like, suppressing a yawn.

Under the sun, he grew more and more lazy. He wished he were in bed still and might have been had Geraldine not interrupted his dreams with all that fuss about phones. It had been like his mother. She was always bursting in in the mornings when he was on the verge of something voluptuous:

'Sex is all your generation thinks about! What about your studies? How can we afford to live now that your father's gone and the pension eaten up by inflation? Get up. Time to be off!'

Nag, nag. Hadn't she ever been young? – Krzysztof decided with vague inadvertence that he couldn't stand women over a certain age. But then he wondered what his poor mother (whom he actually loved) had looked like when twenty, before being overtaken by a husband, child and unending work...

A pair of pert breasts passed by beneath a mauve t-shirt. The face above them was ugly, but the nipples pressed out berry-coloured. They seemed a little miracle of audacity next to the deflated mounds on these aged, other females; and Krzysztof felt himself come up hard again.

Shifting his stance, he tried to disguise it. But against the sheer, sheeny material of his sweat-pants, the thing poked out like a broom-handle; and Ugly Face caught a glimpse. What the hell, he thought: if you're going to be damned, so be it! This kind of weather doesn't last long: get your thrills while you can. So he jumped on a tram behind her.

It was terribly humid. He was wet-hot. It would rain in a while. She glanced back.

Near some students' housing on Lumumba Street, he made out a patch of green. Across the road were some poplars, indicating a park. Jumping off, he headed into some elder bushes by it. If she follows, I'll fuck her, he shocked himself by thinking; but in such heat all shock was muffled.

She did follow, or seemed to. With a half-conscious thrill, Krzysztof watched her jump off the tram a little ways on. Taking a step into a clump of young ash trees, he turned and waited.

Blood thumped in his veins. Her face was pocked and hair mousey. This is degenerate, he thought: she was a reflection from the bottom of the abyss. Yet, he reached out a fingertip and let it touch one of those berry-shaped nipples.

A charge seemed to come from it: electric, energizing. A clap of thunder rolled away in the distance. A gust of warm wind turned the leaves.

'Not so fast, hon,' she said in the *patois* of an American hooker; and pulling out a flick-knife – 'The price first.'

They could hardly believe his story at the 'klub' in the students' tower-block on Lumumba; they believed the slash across his cheek, however. Though not deep, it had splattered blood over his t-shirt; and the trio of girls who filled the place at that hour (Krzysztof recognized one of them from the patio of the state café) found it appealing to fuss over him.

They ran upstairs to get bandages and generally played nurse, chattering all the while. One told a story about how she'd been harassed on a tram for wearing a leather cap at a jaunty angle. 'Where do you think you are?' a man had snarled at her; 'Berlin?' He had been one of the vodka-soaked army of new unemployed, she explained; a few other 'beasts' had growled in chorus, and she had been 'petrified'.

'It's frightful the way things are going here,' the second of the trio said. (They all looked quite prosperous and had enough money, at least one, for coffee here a mere two hours after ice cream at the state café.)

'Poland is going to the dogs,' summarized the third, curling a strand of her will-o'-the-wisp hair.

They went on in aria, duet and trio as Krzysztof sipped the tea they had bought him. Then the one who had been in the state café spied his notebook (the girl in the woods had not bothered to steal it when she'd taken his cash). She snatched it from his hand to see what he'd drawn.

'You must do us now!' she demanded, as if affronted that he had not done her and the others before.

'You may call it the Three Witches,' added the one of the leather cap.

'The Three Good Witches,' qualified the third. 'Not like that one who slashed your pretty face.'

'We won't give you tram-fare back if you don't,' leather-cap warned.

'What were you doing in the woods anyway?' the girl from the state café asked him quite slyly.

Her mock-cross little pout reminded him of Agnieszka. And shortly he had produced a sketch which so gratified them that they decided to 'reward' him by escorting him back to town. ('Must protect you,' leather-cap claimed.) Then when the tram reached the Opera Square, they decided to reward him further by inviting him to a larger park on the outskirts: there he could 'recuperate' in the sun while they studied for upcoming exams.

Krzysztof grew soothed by these flutterings. He did not have to be back for Geraldine till evening; besides, he was fed up with that. He would meet her sometime: he needed money to get to Warsaw, either by himself or as her driver; after that he would be free. The Three Good Witches were a sign: normal life with normal people of his type and age were what he needed now.

Not that he had needed much of a sign. Agnieszka he longed for; and as they settled in a great field in the second park (it was less a park than a wild space of pristine country next to a forest that looked like it had been there since the beginning of time), he told them about her. He did this less to boast than to forestall any thought any one of them might have had about becoming his girl. The fact was that they were all so pretty that he couldn't have chosen between them if some god had required him to; and as the hours stretched out, he joked about marrying all three – not so silly considering how they hated to be apart from one another and with the situation in the East being as it was: people *did* have to stick together to get by, didn't they? He drew a large sketch of the field and a peasant's farm with forest in the background; the girls pretended to study but mostly they giggled and did cart-wheels, throwing up their skirts. It was terribly pretty, and Krzysztof felt a disconcerting rise in his trousers again; but now he was determined to be good.

Thus passed the rest of a long, pre-May afternoon. It was nearly sunset before they made their way back to the haze of the centre. By the Opera Square the sky was dark gold and the House itself – a great Stalinist block as in Warsaw, only smaller – lit up as students like themselves, decked out in finery, flooded in for a performance of *Don Giovanni*. By the tram-stop, a band of denimed musicians loitered carrying lutes, two guitars and a double-bass; and Krzysztof thought, maybe the Rainbow era was at hand after all. Maybe those long summer afternoons of freedom the students enjoyed at Pittsburgh *were* about to come here. He hoped so! But then, after bidding farewell to his protectresses, he started off towards the Grand. And turning down a dim street, he came upon a haggard mother and daughter trying to keep a burly drunk from beating up on a string-bean of a man.

Against the hollow beatitude of night, squeals sounded, punches thumped. The string-bean staggered back and nearly fell into Krzysztof; the burly drunk was held off by the women and a third man who happened on the scene. But this third man was a string-bean too, and the burly one soon broke free, with the result that – just as Krzysztof was offering a handkerchief to the beaten-up man to mop the blood off his face – the burly one rushed them from behind.

The string-bean yelped like a dachshund set on by a mastiff and tore away down the street. Instinctively, Krzysztof tried to block the drunk from following, only to feel a fist into his belly, and in a moment much worse.

*

Geraldine regarded herself as not in Hell quite, but surely in Purgatory. She had nausea, throbbing head, aching bones, wind, all of which she put down to Polish food, air and coffee. Her night had been sleepless: first the *de rigueur* sex with Krzysztof; then attempts to phone London. To whom? Well – to Leoline Hooper.

That surprised her. It was a measure of her fall. She never called Leo: hadn't done so in years. And what would she have said had she got through? 'Oh darling, I'm in trouble, I've done something stupid, come bail me out'? That's how she'd felt, but to have said so wouldn't have done, not unless she'd been raped, beaten and left by the side of the road. Better just, 'O Leo darling, I'm in Poland still, doing an extra lecture. You wouldn't be a lamb and call the department and tell them for me? I don't know who else to turn to at this hour, and the phones here are so bad one can't get through in the day.'

She had felt better settling on this form of words and sat in the yellow-grey of the street-lamp dialling. But with each attempt, she'd got a busy signal; and since the signal wasn't English, she'd worked out that it was the Polish lines that were engaged. Who else would he have been ringing at that hour? – It was a comfort to have him there.

'Oh by the way, darling, my pearls were stolen, the ones you bought me in Siena: heartbreaking, isn't it? I tried to get them back, but…' She might have said this if he'd seemed glad to hear from her; though if he had, it wouldn't have been necessary –

might even have sounded odd to Krzysztof had he wakened, and she had to be careful about that now: the boy's sensitivities mattered too, didn't they? No, she couldn't have used such a phrase unless Leo had sounded off-ish, or she'd sensed there was another woman in his bed. Never wise to fire the heavy artillery unless absolutely essential.

That had been the plan. The execution, however, had been subverted by the unreconstructed phone system. Geraldine had dialled and redialled till her finger had ached. She had asked reception to try – nothing. Finally, after a bribe of sex (she'd no longer been sure he wouldn't have preferred sleep), she'd asked Krzysztof to attempt it for her.

This had been tricky. If Leo had answered, she would have had to grab the receiver and pretend the boy was an operator, an excuse which might have caused offense. In the event, though, he had had no more luck than she. And it had ended with him suggesting they ring the exchange and book a call for 7:30 a.m.

'He'll be gone by then.'

'He?'

'My colleague, at the university. The one who's subbing for me while I wile away the hours with you.'

It was sordid. Why had she lied? And why, having lied, had she felt moved to try to cover up with more sex? Obviously by then he was more tired than lustful. It even struck her that he might have begun to despise her morals: all Poles were self-righteous Catholics, weren't they? or her ageing body: what was the pull of a forty-five year old with big hips when you could have all the tight, young undergraduates you wanted?

The first made her want to stop, turn her face to the wall and be good; the second made her want to have him all the more – to fuck him until he was so sex-addled that he couldn't raise a thought or member for anyone but her! Which reflection, in day-light, struck her as pure evil. What on earth had possessed her, she wondered, hopping in a cab for the Philological Institute.

But she couldn't think about such things now: had to put on the mask – eminent lecturer from the West, guest of so on and so forth. Still, they lurked inside, along with the nausea creeping up. Shame and pity even made her wonder if she didn't love him a little – he was vulnerable, after all, in a way that Leo Hooper was not; and that was an elixir, wasn't it?

Only in her subconscious did Geraldine intuit that this vulnerability might hide certain danger. She had seen his aggression, his near tantrum in the café, but had registered no threat. It had been only natural, she rationalized as the cab pulled up next to a tower in Kościuszko Street. (Vaguely she noted the pride these natives took in naming everything after long-gone heroes.) Women in sex, all animals maybe, wanted to exhaust their partners; it was simply their way of expressing desire, getting the most out of the male, reassuring themselves of primacy in sex and getting pregnant finally...

O my God, she wondered, opening the door: is *that* it?

In the hour and a half since she'd phoned the Institute to announce her arrival, everyone of importance to Eng Lit in Łódź had been summoned. This did not represent an overwhelming number, but paucity in bodies was made up for by eminence in titles and grey hair. There was Professor-Habile Spaliński, bespectacled, eighty, a survivor of the Warsaw Uprising, who had cooperated with the Reds to found the Institute after the War; Prof-Hab Zakrzewska, sixty odd and wearing a hair-piece, who claimed to be a Ruthenian countess and had once chatted with Graham Greene when he had come to Poland as a guest of the Communist-Catholic organization, Pax; Prof Wieczorek-Tatko, bandaged around both ankles as a result of heart-trouble, who spoke of John Keats as if she had met him personally; Docent Gombrowicz, a youngish poet, out of place among these old régime types, who sidled over to Geraldine to ask *sotto voce* if she'd fancy a meal with him afterwards; at last Prof-Hab Dąbrowska, round and sweet-faced, acting head of the zakład (it was she who had invited Geraldine in the first place), who reminded her that she was already scheduled to have lunch with her after – 'So we can get to know one another more freely,' she added, as if liberty of discourse were still in question here.

She sailed through these introductions and settled in a '50s-style armchair in a high-ceilinged office of faded yellows and browns. Here a special talk was about to commence – 'Not yours, alas,' Prof Wieczorek-Tatko lamented; 'We'll have to save that for tomorrow, if you'll agree.' A lesser event had long been on the schedule. But she would be happy for an excuse to spend another day in their fair city, wouldn't she?

Geraldine smiled – what else could one do? – and suppressed the taste of sick creeping up from her tummy.

In addition to dignitaries of the Institute, the office was populated by one student and a married couple from Surbiton who ran an English language teachery down the road. Above a desk hung a portrait of the Queen, the English one, rendered blonde – indeed, nearly transformed into the Slavic iconness of the painting in the Polonia breakfast-room. The scheduled speaker was led in to sit beneath this.

A graduate of Oxbridge, he was introduced as once having taught composition at Łódź; now he had returned from a red-brick job in Britain to share his experiences as a translator of Polish poetry. Bony, lean, with an accent from the Home Counties, this boy, as Geraldine immediately thought him (couldn't have been a day older than Krzysztof), gave off neurosis compared to his audience. Sputtering, fumbling, he began by going into excessive detail about himself, then apologized and altered tack.

His subject was a Polish 'beatnik' poet of the 1950s (she could not catch the name, let alone pronounce it), his theme whether the poet's work and writing of that era overall – Kerouac, Ginsberg and so on, along with their Liverpudlian counterparts – constituted literature truly or just diary-keeping. A dedicated technician, he obviously knew Polish well and the pitfalls of translating it. One of the violin players, she inwardly dubbed him: all the little experts, so pressed and pedantic – the glory and bane of the British system.

From his first words, her mind began to wander; she pictured him at sixty, just as thin, just as sharp. Meanwhile, the old Polish colleagues' minds were straying off too, fantasies of Lithuanian castles mixing with images of blonde English queens. Prof-Hab Spaliński's eyes closed: he seemed to embody a Polish version of the Oblomov syndrome. The lady professors in turn struck her as stuffed exhibits of the *dolce far niente* of the old system: of years of being unchallenged (indeed, unencouraged) to reach intellectual heights. To be here must have been like being in a low security prison, Geraldine mused, blissfully unconscious of how patronizing she was.

Meanwhile, the poor Oxbridger discoursed on 'Situationist Writers'. Asked what this term meant, he referred to great authors who had 'loved listing things that happened and would happen only once': Joyce, for example, Proust, Henry Miller. By writing up an experience, however banal, they added something to it forever: 'perhaps something metaphysical,' he stated. The best had pushed back the limits of what received situations might be, using grammatical anarchy or even made-up words.

'They pushed and pulled the language in order to get a thought through,' he summed up, looking tortured and not remotely up to his task.

The old-timers muttered. Prof-Hab Spaliński woke up with a disapproving grunt. The boy tried to illustrate what he meant by describing the smell of paint in a flat he had visited the previous day and how it had brought back his first sensations on coming to Poland; and Geraldine, touched, recalled something in her own past – or was it more recent? an image of Krzysztof so refreshing amid all that rhetoric at Kraków...

By the time she'd refocused, the poor lecturer was giving off energy in inverse proportion to his audience. Without positive reaction, he seemed to turn on himself. Words came out now as if he were impatient with them; ideas broke into fragments, half-promising sparks, which failed to ignite. The halfness of his constructions seemed to increase his frustration, as did anyone who interrupted his flow, which the others started to do in a genteel crescendo.

Prof Zakrzewska stood up for traditional realist narrative; the boy tried to attack it as *passé* and false, defending the Beats' record of the '50s as 'a lyrical celebration'. Celebration of what? he was asked. 'Of Truth and Enthusiasm,' came the answer, 'even Sentiment!' Magisterial scorn. The Beats had been 'decadent individualists,' Spaliński averred; 'entirely without a sense of responsibility such as had been necessary in Poland in those times!' Others agreed; the boy withdrew into bluster. Such an expense of passion (he was beginning to sweat) and all for just six or eight people!?

For a moment, Geraldine loved her country in him, just as she rather despised it in the Surbiton couple who watched as if interested but would certainly dismiss the event after as an example of 'Oxbridge elitism'. Then, without warning, it all seemed to collapse. Under the Poles' disapprobation, the boy admitted that perhaps his Beats had not been writers at all, just street-persons able to seduce naïve young readers with verbal pyrotechnics. 'Fireworks, not poetry,' a voice iterated – this of Docent Gombrowicz, the acknowledged Authority on such matters, being not only a poet but, more important, the founder of the Solidarity chapter at the Institute. Having spent a year in prison in the early 1980s for publishing *samizdat* books, his views were taken as gospel now, at least in public, even by mastodons of the old régime. In face of his scorn, a novitiate lecturer had little choice but to fold up his tent.

Geraldine went away nauseated slightly more, though in mind perhaps more than body. She had to wonder what she would say to the professors the next day when her turn to talk came. Subconsciously this meant how could she *redeem* them, sainted missionary from the West that she was. But that was vain, her conscious self now chided, having observed at first hand the glee certain Easterners took in humiliating 'friends' from the West.

How could she redeem herself might have been more to the point. For wasn't she part of the problem? – Geraldine had begun to ask herself this by the time she got back to the Grand. Or was it just because she felt so unutterably exhausted that she started to plummet into shame? Krzysztof – how could she have done it? It violated her morals: it violated her self-image to behave as she had. And that was not even to consider what it might have done, or could be doing, to him.

She felt sickened, though less so in the tummy since nausea had migrated to her brain. The glimmer of an idea that she was pregnant for the time being abated, and she lay down to try a restorative nap. But it was too hot, and she too agitated.

Her mind raked over the previous days and what had brought

her to Poland. Cataloguing her responses since arrival, she had to admit that she'd been fed up in London and that, by the conference at Kraków, something inside her had been in full revolt. The very language of English, basis of her profession, had begun to oppress her. Her being had longed to recoil from the speech-centres and brain to the life-centres and womb – thus Krzysztof, thus sex, thus the fix she was in. She had come with her own troubles, dumped them on him and done little good otherwise. The whole business of being a great Western author on ambassadorial mission to the East was a joke: with the money spent on her trip and the conference, an entire block in a city like Łódź might have been run and its inhabitants fed for a year. It was an ego trip, pure and simple: for her, for the organisers, for the native academic establishment which sucked up to them while despising Western intellectuals in private, as the morning's reaction to an untitled young Quixote had underlined.

She would tell the Man from the World Bank – yes! She would give her talk in the morning, go back to Warsaw, debrief her superior and depart. She would spend the next hours preparing Krzysztof. (A twinge told her he would be relieved to see the back of her). But *where was he now*? – To her shock a spasm of heat flushed her womb. And leaping upright, she rearranged her skirts and set off for her scheduled luncheon.

Prof Dąbrowska lived with her husband, a history lecturer, and their son in a high-rise block a short cab ride from the centre. Next to a park, it was not far from a Stalinist opera house similar to the one in the Great Square up in Warsaw.

The day was blisteringly hot by the time Geraldine arrived but the flat dark and cool, with blinds half-drawn against an excessive glare. Ersatz-wooden bookshelves lined the walls, lending a *gravitas* almost ceremonial to the hospitality she was to receive. Wanda, as the good woman was called (Geraldine instantly thought of her as that) led her to table without preliminary. Husband and son being out (the latter would slip in as they ate and vanish into one of the other four rooms that made up the quadrant), the meal was for two.

The main course consisted of barley, white beans from a tin

and small slices of pork rolled with pickle inside, covered with sauce made from cooking juices and soured cream. This was preceded by a white barszcz of sour flour, potatoes and bits of pink sausage, washed down by Polish beer, and followed by orange jelly with cream, which Wanda beat by hand at the table.

'I don't like electrical appliances,' she confided, 'though I can afford them. I prefer to do things in the old way.'

Her voice was as round and reassuring as her shape. Her outlook seemed round and reassuring too. Like most Poles, she was a good Catholic, Wanda explained. But though her husband had prospered under the old régime, she disliked Communism for its lack of freedom and economic naïveté. At the same time, she feared for the future, she said.

These views were expressed as they settled post-prandially for tea on matching settees. And Geraldine noted how different in style her hostess was from counterparts in the West. Each subject was chewed over long and fully, with no straining after cleverness. The narrative line was rich, contemplative, peram-bulatory (tedious, some might say) but at the same time musical. It was easy to see how a new Eastern anxiety might be linked to perceived loss of atmospheres like these.

Under pressure of the new system everything was changing, Wanda mused, not least in academe. Career competition had replaced full employment. Nor did the changes quite mean letting the People have what they wished:

'We still have the habit of receiving ideas from above. Now for a time the Church will be in power; it is not democracy yet as you have in the West – maybe we do not even want that here. Poles in the mass rather deceive themselves with their myths. For instance, we still think of ourselves as "the Christ among nations", a mystical idea put forward by one of our Romantic poets, a dispossessed aristocrat who went to Paris in the '40s of the last century and became the centre of the *émigré* community there. We are, you see, quite hopeless romanticists.'

As the good woman talked, her guest could almost have slept. The largeness of her periods and lullingness of her tone made one believe that, despite what she said, all would come right in the end. So seductive were her words that Geraldine half-decided that she longed to become like Wanda herself. The maternal persona, in such contrast to the jokey-satirical antics of Twitch or *de haut en bas* pronouncements of the Voice at the conference or tortuous technical brilliance yet lack of conviction of the boy from Oxbridge that morning, had an authority all of its own. And wasn't an English version of it, seasoned with lyricism and wit, what Geraldine had been aiming at all these years? Wasn't it what she had almost achieved until Kraków – until, in a word, she had broken her progress with mad sex?

Wanda convinced her all the more without knowing (though who could tell what these people knew: informants and spies had only recently become *passé* in Poland, if they had at all) that she had made a grave mistake. As if to drive the message home, the good woman insisted, following numberless cups of tea, on taking her to the opera ('You are here such a short while, and our culture is under such pressure that it may be your only chance to see what we can do!') So they strolled out in the early evening light towards the centre. And Geraldine came rather quickly to wish that her hostess had not laid on this final 'treat'.

Lunch and talk had been perfect. She longed to go back to the hotel carrying their atmosphere with her and wrap up her Polish interlude, taking herself home on something which felt like a virtuous path. But the opera partly negated her hostess's contention that something of worth had existed under the old régime. It was *Don Giovanni* and the production the most lamentable Geraldine could have conceived of.

Though respectable in its way, the house seemed to be swarming with teenagers made to come by their parents but longing for rock-and-roll just as much as their forbears in the West circa 1969. Whispering and giggling, they left their seats during crucial arias. Perhaps because the price of a ticket was a one-hundredth of what it would have been at Covent Garden, the sanctity of the event seemed non-existent to them. Nor was it just students who were infected with slackness. The singers and set left an impression like people like the Man from the World Bank were inclined to: that this was a second or third rate European nation which didn't know what it was up to.

Ersatz Parisian or Viennese elegance pervaded costumes and

gestures. The director had made no effort to relate the story to the situation of the East after Communism's fall, as one might have in, say, Berlin. As for the matter of sex, in which the story was drenched in every character from the Don to the peasant Zerlina, there was nothing to put faith in: the women were coquettes, the men mere players at a *machismo* which showed no sign of being native. It was voyeurism of what the new East thought it should be, given for students who had no incentive to stick it out. And by the end the cavernous theatre was half empty (it had begun full) so that Geraldine was perhaps the sole viewer left to be shocked by the production's signal innovation:

Instead of Mozart's vigorous, ironic coda in which all the survivors sing a paean to virtue and reform, the tableau was cut off, leaving a ragged limb as it were, at the moment of the libertine's being dragged down to Hell.

The effect was macabre. Strangely upset by it, our lady made her niceties to her hostess and fled to a cab. On Wanda's direction, the driver wheeled off for the Grand, leaving Geraldine to sit back into swelling trepidation about how she was going to handle her own amorous victim for a last night. Then forward motion was halted by a fracas in the street.

Several people were engaged in a pitched battle, it seemed. Irritably, she leaned up to persuade the driver to reverse, veer around or do one of the feats of derring-do London cabbies are so schooled in; but her Polish was not up to it. (Its non-existence was a main reason she had been supplied with a personal driver in the first place). And so as the cab idled, waiting for strife to climax in death or whatever it portended (where were those thuggish police when you needed them, she mused), she was forced to train eyes on the terror in process. And focusing, she realized that the head bouncing like a bloody football off the boot of the main assailant belonged to Krzysztof Robiński.

II.

The Antinomians

The relative weakness or strengths of institutions of a
newly formed free society is only one aspect of the whole
issue. What about the people? Are they ready for such a
rapid change? Does free society presuppose in addition
to the creation of its basic institutions some set of values
or moral standards that would properly anchor the
society? Do the people need an interim period of
schooling? Is such schooling realizable? Are there
teachers for such procedure? Are the people willing to be
educated?

My answer to these and similar questions is rather
simple. The people are always ready and they do not
need a special education. What they need is a free space
for their voluntary activities, the elimination of controls
and prohibitions of all kinds.

—Vaclav Klaus, first premier of the Czech Republic

Leoline Hooper had decided it was time for action. He did not
know what he was walking into, however. The first
indication was the LOT flight to Kraków. The compartment was
packed tight; around him sat a collection of Hasidic Jews, old
men and old-looking youths, bearded, intent, falling asleep over
their Torahs. A large man with an American accent was annoyed
at being seated among them; after the plane took off, he got up
and went to the rear cabin, muttering loudly that it was

completely empty back there. Eventually, Leo went to explore and discovered the man occupying a row to himself. He had kicked forward the seats in front of him so that he could stretch out his legs.

'Always herd us like cattle in three rows on these flights. Scared the damn Ilyushin jets won't make the take-off 'f there's too much weight in the rear.'

Leo stretched out his own considerable length in a seat opposite. The man took this as a sign to keep talking. (Actually, he half-yelled over the sound of the engines.) He was a maker of plastic bags, he explained. Came from Chicago, north side. And what did Leo do, and why he was going to Poland?

Geraldine's ex got out the first half of an answer before the man interrupted:

'Poland's ideal for investing in real estate and creating shopping-malls. But,' he added, half-nodding at a blonde stewardess, 'watch out for these people.'

'Why's that?' Leo queried.

'Ever seen one of these?'

The man pulled up his shirt-sleeve. Under the forearm was a number comprised of several digits. It looked like a brand burnt into a chunk of wood.

'Know what that is?' he demanded surprisingly fiercely.

It turned out that he was a survivor of Auschwitz. Norman Niemenstein was his name, and he was coming to Poland on an annual visit as a board-member for a 'march of the living'. This took place every year to commemorate the day on which the death-camp had been liberated.

Oscillating between friendly advice and outbursts of spleen, Norman occupied Leo's consciousness for the rest of the flight. In reference to the Hasids up in front, he exclaimed that if the world were not willing to insure the survival of Israel he hoped 'someone would have the guts to blow it to Kingdom Come!' This kind of outburst Leo had sometimes made for effect at boring parties in north London which Geraldine had dragged him to. But Norman 'meant business', and it was sobering.

By the time they touched down, Leo was trying to figure out how to slip away from his new 'friend'. The airport at Kraków was tiny, however; so they ended up sharing a cab into town. During the trip, Norman regaled him further with potted opinions on Poland, most of which Leo ignored. One that stuck with him was about a town the man pronounced as 'Woodge':

'That's where you should go; everyone avoids it. Germans and Austrians 'll own Kraków in five years; Warsaw's got entrepreneurs over it like flies on shit. Łódź is the ticket. Built in the golden age of the last century: Jewish finance, German engineering, Polish labour – the perfect mix. Old Commie factories gone to pot now; need to be retooled for light industry, shops. If I was Mr Big making a master-plan for this place, that's where I'd send a go-ahead guy like you... By the way, here's m' card, 'case you ever get to Chicago. I got friends who'd be happy to do business with you: dentists and so on with a little spare cash. They're too old now to come over themself, but...'

Leo gazed out the window. It was one of those days of mid-spring which are sunny but unseasonably cool.

'Polar ice-cap's melting,' Norman went on like the village explainer. 'Makes for strange weather in this part a the world. And when it melts enough so's real summer can come, brother then it is hot!'

The sun shone through a haze of pollution, making it look like a poached egg. The driver deposited them near a place called the Florianska Gate. Approaching it, Norman mused:

'Never been here before? Gotta see this. First sight of this square is one of the great experiences of travel in Europe, they say. Maybe anywhere.'

Strolling past a 19th century, Parisian-style opera house, they passed beneath the brick ramparts of a medieval wall. A few steps further on, they turned into a narrow, pedestrian street flanked by grand-ish hotels.

'There's the Podroża; 's the best. 's where the French writer Balzac' (he pronounced it 'Ballsack') 'stayed on his way to see his girlfriend near L'wów. That's in Ukraine now. You can almost hear the carriages clattering over the cobblestones, huh? just like in an old film.'

As if on cue, a horse-drawn buggy passed, but without 'Ballsack' in it, or anyone other than a driver looking as haggard as his horse. Ambling behind it, the travellers emerged into the great square. And here Leo was indeed impressed.

'Nothing like it except San Marco in Venice,' Norman was saying; but Leo had not been to Venice, so for him it evoked Siena, which brought to mind Geraldine, and his reason for being there. 'Maybe a touch of Nuremburg to it too, or Munich – people say so. Don't know myself; never had the stomach for Germany, tho' I hear it can be picturesque. Architecturally, this place is a cross between the Italian Renaissance, the Bohemian baroque and the Viennese Imperial of what they call "la belle époque" in France. That's when my people came here, from Pińsk in White Russia. Chased out by Tsarist pogroms. Began with a stall over there, in the Sukkierne, that big, arched market-hall where merchants used to come in the Middle Ages to sell silk from the East. Worked their way up to having a house over there, behind the Cathedral. Yeah, that one. 's where the present Pope used to be archbishop of.'

Leo felt a genuine lift of the spirit. How sane-making it was to travel! He almost thanked Geraldine in his mind for having provoked him to this precipitate chase. He had needed a break. London without her had become so ingrown, and nothing could damage your state of mind more than workaholic routine in that pressure-cooker. (Was *that* what had gone wrong between them?) … He found himself staring at a pair of young lovers lounging arm-in-arm under a statue, which Norman identified as of Adam Mickiewicz. This brought to mind strolling around the piazza in Siena and what doting doves they had been then. It was a day when Leo had spent all his money (something he had never done with anyone since) to buy her a long string of pearls.

Norman had persuaded him to sit at one of the tables outside of the Sukkierne. The man looked younger than his years, Leo thought: Americans often did. Breathless, this one had to be over sixty – possibly suffering from high blood-pressure too.

'I'm on my way to the Holiday Inn,' he puffed. 'Old Commie hotels'll be fine soon as they're privatized. At the moment you can't rely on 'em.' – And where was Leo going? just touring?

Instinctively, Geraldine's ex admitted to no more than that.

He had a plan, of course: his pursuit had been sketched out in London, with Professor Twitch. But if Geraldine were really lolling with some Polish chauffeur *in flagrante* as that old gossip maintained, Leo was ambivalent about catching her at it. If the novelty hadn't worn off, it might lead to a fight, and she hated violence of whatever kind, she always claimed. Besides, Leo had no right to her as such: his sole purpose was to be around to catch her if she fell, which he felt sure she would. Something in her nature had always made him believe that she would turn back to him in the end – to his superior practicality.

Norman had ordered two beers.

Sipping, they sat watching the scene as it passed.

Apart from the lovers beneath Mickiewicz, there were teenagers in sunglasses, tourists with backpacks, a juggler and group of South American street musicians playing pipe-and-drums to a crowd gathered by a little chapel at the far end of the square. Beyond this, you could just glimpse a spire, which Norman identified as tip of the chapel of the Wawel Castle, which stood on a promontory overlooking the city and the valley of the Wisła below. But Norman was less interested in tour-guiding now. Explaining the hardships Westerners encountered in trying to reclaim assets here, he pointed to a smudge on the far side of the square and told of how a merchant family from Toronto had recently regained possession of their old town-house, only to have it fire-bombed.

'See what problems we still have?'

Leo's gaze had gravitated to another pale blonde like the one on the plane. Alertly, his companion shifted tack:

'Never could read Polish women myself. Maybe you'll have better luck at it.'

'That's not what I'm after,' Geraldine's ex snapped.

'Course not. Still, a little joy never hurt. Look how she walks, as if she was a countess. They all have these aristocratic pretensions – pathetic! They're never going to make it; still, they put it out. This whole country's problem is false pride.'

In addition to gilded youth and a street-carnival atmosphere, a number of drunks and derelicts seemed to lurk about; and Leo began to reassess his impressions. As Norman talked on, the property-developer in him reflected on how poorly the buildings seemed to be maintained – even the churches. It was as if the smoky air and battered state of the people had demoralized the very stones. 'Liberty requires energy,' Norman was saying as Leo noted how lethargy seemed to affect even the young in their ersatz Levi's – this in contrast to what he had known in his own shopping-malls back in London. The lovers seemed glued by their bottoms to Mickiewicz's plinth; the obvious habitués of the café gazed vacantly outwards, as if their only true vision were an inner emptiness. 'Unemployment really terrible now,' Norman was saying as an ancient thing on crutches and with one leg came swinging through the tables towards them:

'You American?' he grumbled in broken English.

Gap-toothed, stubble-faced, he was no picture-postcard, and Norman pointedly ignored him.

'You American?' he repeated.

The question was not hostile, only insistent, yet Norman was clearly non-plussed. Leo got the impression that the old-timer, perhaps mutilated in the war, was one of those types you saw in Turkey and Greece who made a living by sidling up to 'friends' from the Land of the Brave and the Free who had supposedly helped their country throw off its oppressors.

'You American?' a third time, poking a finger into Norman's shoulder.

It was perhaps no more than a prelude to soliciting *baksheesh*; nor did any other customer take notice. The waitress did not try to shoo the man away, as might have happened in the West. Even so, Norman's face went tormented:

'Tell the guy to buzz off!' he gasped.

It seemed too minor an incident to get upset over. Still, Geraldine's ex intervened:

'Yes, he's American. Now please, if you want money, here. But leave us in peace.'

The ancient thing cast hardly a glance at the change Leo had fished from his pocket. 'Real American?' he went on at Norman. 'Or *Jew*?'

'See what I mean?' the Auschwitz survivor demanded.

'OK shove off now!' Leo murmured and, turning the ancient

thing around, sent him on his way, saying back, 'He's harmless enough.'

'Don't you believe it!' – Norman slammed his own coins on the table and rose on unsteady pins. 'The War never ended here – not for us, or for them. You watch out, son. And if you need help, call me. You got my card.'

With that he set off across the square, jostling people out of his way as if their only intention in being there had been to obstruct his progress.

Sad creature, our Londoner was left to muse. Soon, though, he had put the scene out of mind – it was somebody else's problem, wasn't it? – and looking at his watch, he realized he had to get a move on himself if he wanted to reach his destination – the Instytut Filologi of Uniwersytet Jagiellońska – before the teaching day was over.

.

Krzysztof was hazy about how he had come to be in this comfortable, Alpine-style house in the woods. The Englishwoman had told him, but he'd been too punch-drunk to hear. Before she'd gone out, she'd put some złotys on the table beside him:

'Take it easy, dear boy. I'll be back as soon as I can.'

His head was hurting. Not surprising – it was swathed in bandages. He could hardly recall what had happened. And where was his car?

There was sun in the leaves. He felt Agnieszka's presence beside him as he trudged through blonde grass. Happy, peasant-like, he was a young man on a sunny day in Poland, or perhaps anywhere anytime. Who cared where he was or who?

Birds were cawing. A pair of rooks dive-bombed a stork in a tree-top. But it was too late here for rooks, wasn't it? Didn't they fly back to Siberia, or wherever, by this season?

It was warm in the field, but cool under the leaves.

The rooks kept circling, cawing. Had they come back just to harass these sparrows and the stork?

Cries of children on swings, barks of dogs, footfalls, susurrus of walkers, cars and busses whisking by... No: that was Warsaw.

There were no busses here, not at the edge of these woods.

The caws sounded like joy, or like war. Rooks were the only creatures who thrived here in winter, though it was not that season now... Entering the sun, he saw a field in the distance. Across it, teenagers played on top of a hill. They had started a fire; now it was burning out of control. In the quickening breeze, it hissed at them fiercely as they tried to beat it down with their coats. Another gust from behind and it would sweep it down the hill like a *Blitzkrieg*. So Krzysztof ran up.

Tearful, apologetic, they must have thought him quite frightening as he swooped down on them like some great rook flapping wings. Beating the flames back with his own jacket, he scattered them as if the sparrows or stork. At last it was smothered: only smoke and black earth. Meanwhile, from far away on the road, they stood staring at him as if he were some monster silhouetted against the sun: a Frankenstein's monster, head stitched and swathed in mummy-like skeins.

Had they run away from him out of fear or of shame? He could hardly say as one waved back sheepishly. Was it in thanks? Coughing a little, he loped down the hill, thinking how his bandaged head hurt.

'Lovely day, isn't it?' the woman kept saying.

Where were they now? another Alpine-style building: restaurant on the fringe of the woods. How had he got here? Where had she come from? – Must not have got as far away as he'd planned.

'Let's have some lunch,' she'd said. 'I'm famished.' So now they were seated at this table with a blue-checked cloth, the only guests in the chalet-like place.

The barmaid had turned up the music when they'd come in – rock-music, British; yet she hadn't liked it. 'Can't you turn that down?' she'd asked of the waitress when she'd brought menus. Krzysztof didn't like it either, but they were only trying to make the place 'fun'. The Englishwoman didn't want 'fun' now, though; she wanted to talk about her lecture that morning and the professors she'd met. But even with the music down, Krzysztof could not quite take it in. Her talk was too animated; his head hurt. At last she seemed to get discouraged.

'Where were you coming from when I met you?' she asked. 'You shouldn't've gone so far alone.'

He explained how he'd had to put out a fire. She looked at him as if he were losing his mind. Well, maybe he was a bit crazed; he *did* feel pretty odd. The music was too loud still, but he couldn't compound her rudeness by saying so. The waitress and barmaid looked quite pretty, though like everyone else they were beginning to age.

'You should go back to bed,' the Englishwoman advised.

Bed? – No, he didn't want that. The word itself sounded like suffocation.

'I'd rather go out there,' he nodded towards the window.

'Yes, lovely day, isn't it? All right. After you've cleaned your plate. But we mustn't go far.'

'Why not?' – And why was she speaking to him as if he were a disconsolate five-year-old?

'My poor battered Pole!' she sighed sadly, laying a hand on his where it lay by a knife.

Her eyes looked pinched. There were streaks of black peeping through the frosting of her bangs. She was as old as his mother, he realized and recalled now the fix he was in.

'Professor Spaliński told me this morning that this was part of the primeval northern European forest,' she said as they trudged through the leaves.

Lunch had made him energetic. She had to keep repeating, 'Slow down!' They were deep in a birch wood, no sign of human life, no field nor hut nor pile of cut logs, only green shoots underfoot and pale buds overhead. She dogged his footsteps, just audibly out of breath. Before she could violate the silence again, he said, 'Ssssh!'

Up in the treetops there had been a crack – tap of woodpecker, cry of a second bird, all else still. A slight buzzing of insects, the smells of the forest – then came a quick, clomping sound and, through the corner of an eye, he caught sight of a boar. Startled by their presence, it disappeared into the northwestern perimeter of trees.

Geraldine put a hand on one of his arms. 'What was it? a bison? Spaliński said there were some of them here too.'

'No, further out. The Białowieża, next to Russia.'

'Is it safe?'

Now she was the child-like one, and it was irritating. Shrugging her hand off, he muttered, 'Of course!' though neither knowing or caring, just wild to be free.

She fell in step again, chin angled to sky, hands deep in the pockets of her corduroy skirt. They passed a small shrine where people came for a drop of spring-water meant to be sacred. One or two monks passed, hands deep in their habits but faces angled towards sandalled feet. On the far side of an amber-black pond, a monastery flickered in and out of view. Then they were lost in a wild wood of birches and half-dead evergreens.

Krzysztof walked more deliberately now. He felt dizzy again. It wasn't unpleasant but made him want just to stop, listen and feel. Gazing up, he saw a diamond of blue over the swaying, silvery tips of the trees. It was utterly still here – as if he'd arrived at the centre of the world. No one was around nor any sound any longer, not even of the dead woman following him.

Pulling down the elastic top of his trousers, he let out a luxuriant pee. A waft of warm breath seemed to blow through the forest. Shaking himself dry, he seemed to hear Nature speak. For a time he stood frozen, penis in hand, ears pricked up to listen. The spell subsiding, he noticed her skirts swishing the needles behind him. Her voice asked:

'Are you alright? Don't you think we should turn back?'

It made him feel angry, or worse. Snapping the elastic back into place, he sensed rage hovering. Tearing off the last blood-stained shred of his clothes, he saw himself racing off through the forest, away from her, away from civilization and all it represented – like that boar disappearing to the northeast.

His head pulsed. His arms and thighs ached with their bruises. He started to walk again. She repeated, 'Slow down!' But he was off now, arousal returning.

He seemed to see Agnieszka, or someone like her, flitting ahead through budding leaves. Laughing and naked, white-skinned, a sprite, she led him on – or was it the three of them from the day before scattering out in several directions, throwing their skirts up, tossing them off until they scampered free? Impulsive, innocent, delighted young animals, they danced away into a warm enwombment of trees.

'Slow down!' the voice cried. 'You're not well, Krzysztof!'

Mother's words, English tones, Western socialization – had to get! Had to dash, merge away into forest, hide somewhere to the east!

Tearing the clothes off, he grew Pan-like. Running, he wondered: should I turn and reveal what a true spirit of Nature thinks of her rationalist-feminine lust for control? Yes, that would shock her! And isn't it what she wants too in some deep fantasy? for me to crouch in the bushes and, once she's caught up, leap out like a lynx and show her what life in the primeval forest might mean? – So he hid in the ferns.

They felt wonderfully tingling against his thighs. Breathing throatily, he thought: is this madness?

'Where are you, Krzysztof?' she called.

Had she been right to look at him as if he'd lost his mind?

'Don't play games with me now. You're not well, and I'm worn out. Let's go back to the hostel: it's going to be hard enough to find our way.'

Then he leapt. Both let out screams, but for different reasons. And as the sound split the stillness of the afternoon, the world went black for him again.

•

Geraldine Scott was stupefied – first afraid for herself; then for him; finally, as his eyes opened and he seemed to regain consciousness, about what to do.

For a time, she just sat there cradling his head in her arms where they'd crashed down in the bluebells and twigs. Vaguely he smiled when she asked if he were OK. The smile turned to a half-chuckle, as if post-coital, though it had hardly been that. He was not in his alarming satyr state any longer, and it was the last thing on her mind.

Was this an error? Should she have made love to him there on the spot? Might it have jostled something back into place? Geraldine by this point could not think about it. The rage for sex which had come on her after Kraków seemed as remote now as a prior life. Had she aged overnight? Her mind was rational again: morally 'sound': a middle-aged English academic's: the same which had charmed the old ladies of Łódź that morning with remarks on 'the Transformational Role of the Heroine in the (sic) 19th Century British Fiction'. Yet here was this sick, naked boy in her arms.

Having dispensed with her Jekyll and Hyde persona, Geraldine felt pity for him, as well as shock. What else was there to do but get him dressed and go for help? The thought of stripping her own clothes off didn't arise. Even in her Hyde persona of previous days, nudity in the open wouldn't have done. Such things were all very well in novels of D. H. Lawrence; but despite the fact that she had got her higher degree in the 1970s, Professor Scott had never equated the cult of a phallic 'dark god' with anything other than literary posturing.

Not that she thought of herself as a prude. Far from it. It was a testament to her liberal-mindedness, wasn't it, that she could rise so readily to the occasion of finding the boy's underpants and putting them back on, as if a clean nappy on an infant who's just thrown a gop of poo in mummy's eye?

'Now pull yourself together and sit by this tree,' she admonished, tugging his trousers up.

He smiled inanely. It was most worrying. Thank God she'd never had a drunk for a husband, nor any man for that matter. And in fact in this moment Geraldine may have become reconciled at last to her status as single female.

Setting him against a birch trunk, she concluded:

'I'm going for help now; you're not to follow. You must sit here till I come back: you have concussion and need to be treated. I don't know what Wanda was thinking when she said you needn't go to hospital. That is exactly where you belong!'

She set out.

Like many an English person of her type, Geraldine did not have compass sense. This may seem odd in a race which, more than any other of modern times, conquered the globe; but there it is. Geographical studies may have been urged in the Victorian era, but by the time Geraldine had been at school, they were a subject one read only if one couldn't get on with anything more glamorous. Literature had been the premier diploma in her day: Leavis had been alive still; *Lady Chatterley*'s trial was fresh; an existential efflorescence meant that a myriad of new expressionisms were blossoming – sociology, psychology, futurology, so on. Literature had eventually subsumed the lot. Which was perhaps why now, in its decadence, literary studies had disappeared into 'theory'.

But these had been the morning's reflections, she thought. Here necessity was at hand, and without compass sense she had trouble recalling a thing about these trees. She tried to gauge west, but the sun had climbed high; and even with a knowledge she didn't possess, finding her way by that method would have been chancy. She might have stayed with Krzysztof long enough to see where it began to descend, though there was no guarantee that that would have made any difference. Despite the techniques of mnemonics she'd long trained herself in, our lady professor could not for the life of her recognize which stand of young birches they had traipsed through.

Re-envisioning the monastery, she tried to make for it. Though not religious (like most of her kind, she was of a vaguely George Eliotic, Virginia Woolfish humanist type), she had a sense that the monks might be willing to help. Wanda's sympathy mixed in with this: the good woman's advice in caring for Krzysztof had reassured her, as had her insistence that they go to the hostel in the woods rather than back to the Grand. ('Such unpleasant people around there these days!') And Geraldine had been relieved too that Wanda had chosen to shield her from gossip by stipulating to the hostel over the phone that she and her driver would need separate rooms.

The woman's authority and *sang-froid* were sustaining as she made a path through the leaves. No longer so conscious of her exhaustion, she even began to fantasize herself into that sort of Brit meant to come out in a crisis. Practical matters had to be faced: the boy had to be got to hospital quick! Arranging such priorities in mind, Geraldine began to intuit as well, just below consciousness, that these events might have a useful aspect: once he was in care, she needn't feel awkward about leaving the country. Wanda could put her on a train up to Warsaw; the Council could book her a flight to London; all that would be left would be for her to make a few polite phonecalls back expressing concern for his condition.

So she calculated, winding through groves. Yet no such calculation could make any landmarks appear. The monastery was not where she had judged it, nor was the time to get there anything like as short as it had taken to get from where they'd come from. Of course they'd walked fast – Krzysztof in his frenzy had kept racing on – and this reassured her somewhat. But the simple fact was (increasingly she could not disguise it) that Geraldine Scott was becoming hopelessly lost.

Round and round she wound until, after a beleaguering spell, she sensed the thickets beginning to thin. Away in the distance she saw a field; to the left where the sun appeared to be edging down stood a row of wooden cottages, three of them, quite small. Approaching these, she discovered that they were no more than shacks, two utterly unused, the third with a cheap aluminium chair in front of it, on which nobody sat.

Discouraged, she carried on.

Bending back towards the edge of the forest, then straightening and angling towards a paved road, the track delivered her to where a dog's bark suggested near-civilization. Going towards it, she wound round a last stand of beech trees and arrived at a roadhouse with bus-stop opposite.

The owner of the bark was stationed at the door of this square cement structure, growling, head down.

'Nice boy,' she murmured, too intent to be scared.

An indecipherable mix of Eastern breeds, it let her pass with reluctance, hackles raised.

Inside, it was dark and cool. Only by this change did Geraldine recognize how oppressively bright the outer world had been. The new atmosphere soothed. Low-ceilinged and spartan, a simple front room brought to mind some white-trash den of the

American south. A Slavic version of country music droned from invisible speakers; flies buzzed, listless; a second dog lay by a cooler where a few bottles of Pepsi and cartons of ice-cream were displayed.

Behind this stood a surprisingly urban-looking woman, thirty odd. In front of her sat a younger woman, smoking. To one side stood an exotic-looking man, dressed as if he had been out hunting. He held a rifle, or maybe it was a shotgun – Geraldine was not up on this Scottish laird sort of thing.

'I'm sorry,' she said and for the first time noted a taint of pretention in her tone. 'Does anybody here speak English?'

Inadvertently, she felt herself slipping into a rôle out of *A Passage to India* – or to shift the allusion to what her sudden precariousness made it seem, that, like Blanche Dubois in *A Streetcar Named Desire*, she had nothing to rely on but the kindness of strangers. Fortunately, the strangers seemed to be just that: kind. The woman at the counter half-smiled and looked to the woman who smoked. This second woman, who had something familiar to her – hair mousey, glasses thick-rimmed – half-smiled as well, though with more irony. She seemed academic and not much older than Krzysztof. Had Geraldine seen her at her talk that morning?

This second woman looked to the man with the gun. He had a face as broad as the Eurasian plain. Weathered yet regal, with high cheekbones and almond-shaped eyes, it put one in mind of landscapes with names like Samarkand and 'the Roof of the World'. Neither Chinese nor Indian, he must have come from some place in the ex-Soviet Union, though Geraldine had no knowledge by which to say where.

'What do you think, Kirsan?' the girl asked in impeccable, if slightly Americanized, English.

Kirsan did not answer. He just stared at the guest until she wondered if he might be a mute.

'I know you,' the girl added. 'I saw you last week at the conference at Kraków. Ridiculous business!'

'I'm sorry.' – On instinct, our lady stiffened. 'I met so many people there; I'm not sure I – '

'We didn't meet as such. You came to my talk. And I made a

manifestation at the last plenary session. That pompous Voice wanking on about things he doesn't have any practical sense of – I was the one who challenged him on the benefits of his so-called "Post-modernism". Everyone else was too polite to speak out, but they all agreed with me.'

'Yes?' – She felt a rictus of geniality spread over her features, though she could only recall these events from afar.

The girl chuckled. 'Fancy you turning up here!'

Into the silence, the cooler hummed.

'Yes,' the Englishwoman repeated, a tingle of fear skewering up her spine, which, through a practised act of will, she did not let drive the colonial authority out of her tone. 'I'm afraid I've lost my way in the forest. The boy who was leading me has taken ill. I was wondering if you possibly had a telephone?'

※

Jagiellonian University's administrative buildings were in a medieval *cul-de-sac* off the Great Square. The Philological Institute, however, was in another part of Kraków outside the walled city; and its character was sharply different. Elegant 19th century villas gave way to shoddy 1960s high-rises. In one of these Leoline Hooper found what he was looking for: the English departmental office.

Staff and students had cleared off, it being past 3:30; the departmental secretary was the only one there. An attractive brunette, she did not fill Leo with optimism as she explained that the conference had been over for three days and the last of the foreign lecturers, a famous Slav *émigré*, whose name meant nothing to him, had departed the previous night.

'Ah,' Leo grunted, uncharacteristically at a loss.

'Is there something I can help with?' she enquired, smiling prettily and arranging a purple shawl over her shoulders.

She wore crimson lipstick and evidently wanted to be seen as 'fun' in the new Western fashion.

'I'm trying to locate one of the lecturers,' Leo muttered, feeling annoyed at himself for having set out so precipitously.

'She was supposed to be back in London two days ago, but we got a message saying she was still here.'

The departmental secretary hesitated. 'Do you mean that you've travelled all the way to Poland just to find her?'

It did sound rash for a middle-aged man. 'Do you have any idea where she's gone?' he asked somewhat crossly.

The secretary now stood away from her desk. As it passed from her lips, her smile seemed to suffuse a body she knew to be not unattractive. Casting an eye over her questioner, she made him recognize two things: that prosperous Westerners must seem like gold-dust to these people, and that women worldwide will respond to a man who sets off at a moment's notice to track down an errant beloved.

'You must mean Professor Scott,' she said. 'Actually, I don't.'

She was dressed in black knits and knee-high boots. Not yet thirty, she had not quite grown stout in what Leo supposed to be a normal Slav manner. One of her knees angled in over the other, suggesting Botticelli's 'Venus Rising Out of the Waves'. Perched on her notional shell, she seemed to be trying to hide from full view the treasures held between her thighs.

'Would you like me to phone the local British Council lecturer? Maybe he would know something.'

'I don't want to put anyone out,' Leo mused, a familiar stand-offishness in tone. 'I should've rung before coming.'

One of her eyes, which was slightly protuberant, seemed to go out of focus. 'It is no trouble. I could try the Council in Warsaw if you prefer. They would know where she is, surely.'

Would they? Not if she had run off. And was it wise to let Geraldine's minders know someone was trying to find her? She would be furious if word got around that an ex-boyfriend was chasing after her like a nanny. If she *were* having a dirty few days with some rabbit somewhere, it might blow her cover. That might affect her career, and Leo was far too much of a careerist himself to risk any such consequence.

'I don't know. Maybe we should just leave it.'

'As you wish.'

She put on a black cloak and offered to help him find his way back to the Rynek, or Great Square.

They passed threadbare shops in the gloaming, and Leo grew more conscious of how rash it had been to have come here. In the grim light, he sensed some existential crossroads beginning to loom up. A realization had been growing on him for some time now that he was going to have to do what his women never tired of saying he ought to: take 'a good look at' himself. The idea rose half-conscious, with vague nausea and a feel of aching bones, as if he were coming down with 'flu. Ordinarily Leo's response to 'flu would be to resist it, nor in this case did he depart from the norm. Letting the secretary (she was called Iwanka) take him in hand, he pretended he had no other choice.

'We shall go to a café in the Sukkierne; that is where the Council man goes. If he is not there, perhaps some professor or student will be. One of them may have heard of your friend.'

He nodded assent, though now his mind was scuttling away from a spectre which was his great fear: that Geraldine Scott did not want him anymore. This was a truth he had been trying to avoid for years; given as much, it had been near folly to have reacted to Twitch's suggestion by having flown here. (What had *that* stirrer-and-shaker's motives been anyway?) Such gestures might be apt when you were thirty and sure your passion was returned; but when you were forty and the woman had long since shut her legs and decamped to the fortress of a new flat, the real question was how to pull your socks up and get on.

So Leo brooded. Meanwhile, his companion rearranged her shawls over her shoulders and, strolling beside him with a prideful sway, swivelled her eyes his direction. Smiling a touch intimately, she gave the impression that she could read more than she let on, which maybe she could. A woman with an agenda is always probing below the surface, Leo knew. From his years of casual liaisons since Geraldine, he knew this as well as he knew the price of square footage in Docklands. Indeed, the situation was almost as normal for him as sitting on his sofa in Cantelowes Square staring at the TV.

'Maybe it would be better just to fly back to London,' he muttered.

'But, you have only just arrived here!'

'I had a free day today. Tomorrow's different.'

She looked at him as if this were some kind of joke. 'You must be very well-off.'

He let that pass.

'Here we are,' she added, leading him into the great Cloth Hall and inside the same café he had sat outside of with Norman an hour before.

It was a good space in an exceptional building in one of the most unique locations in Europe, he thought. Evidently Iwanka thought it quite posh: the way she tugged at her dress in front of the mirror by the cloak stall suggested they might run into the Pope. On further penetration, though, Leo saw that the rooms built into the successive arches had suffered from years of neglect. The cream paint was chipped and gilt edgings looked like lipstick smeared on the cheeks of a tart; the mirrors inlaid into the walls had so many scratches on them that his shaved face appeared to have sprouted a beard; the wallpaper itself was peeling in the upper corners, while the ceiling, adorned with old frescos of cupids against blue-pink heaven, had turned purgatorial with a century of smoke. Still, it was strangely impressive: memorable, at any rate. It had potential, which is what Leo looked for in a space; also something Geraldine had doted on when viewing some half-destroyed Piero della Francescas in churches outside of Siena –

'Pathos,' he breathed.

'I don't see him,' Iwanka replied; and, when he looked at her oddly – 'The Council lecturer.'

'Ah. Not to worry. Just as well.'

'But there are some students at that table there. Would you like to join to them? I can arrange it.'

'Never mind. Let's just sit. I'll buy you a drink. You've been very kind.'

She gave an *aren't-we-having-fun* sort of laugh. 'It is no trouble to help an attractive man who has come all this way to our country. But it would be a pity if he should want to leave again when he has only just arrived.'

Was this to be his fate? to be forever attractive to women of a certain kind? to be subject always to their plots to tame him, 'arrange' him, make him stop, settle, spend his money and be taught what they imagined he'd missed? It never ceased to amaze Leo how quickly a new female could try to direct him. It had to do with genes doubtless, or some biological urge mixed up in the training of children. That would explain why it grew more pronounced the further they got past thirty.

When they were in their twenties, they were girls unless married or with babies, in which case they were marred – 'far too young', as Geraldine used to say when he'd proposed to her at that age. By the time they were forty, they were becoming bossy whether mothers or not; either way they were likely to be tainted by faint bitterness. That's why it was around thirty that they were ripest, in Leo's view. And being ripe, they would be hunters, if free. Ergo this one's evident interest.

Over coffee, she asked him to tell 'all about' himself; he responded with customary reticence; her protuberant eye went out of focus. Once coffee was finished, she asked him for a glass of wine; he ordered it politely, though already twitching to be gone. The wine was cheap, sweet vermouth: quite sick-making if you were working up to the fare of some Covent Garden wine bar. Never mind. It was no more irritating than to have this foreign woman whom he didn't know making observations about how 'shut off' he was.

Presumably, she had tried one or two Englishmen before – possibly even this 'Council lecturer' she'd brought him to the café to find. In any case, as she chattered, Leo felt his spirit rove, as it did when he felt caught in some small social trap.

Not unattracted to beauty, he often found himself drawn by a cheekbone or lip if it could conjure the absent beloved. Some- times at parties where the usual form was the back-biting people took up when at a loss for a subject, he would fix on a feature and fall into a trance. His gaze would rest there until the feature's owner could only assume that he fancied her like mad and contrive to get him her mobile phone-number before leaving. This is how Leo had gained a reputation of being a womaniser. But in this setting, as his eye traversed an epic painting of the Jagiellonian court – quite dramatic in subject though second- rate Delacroix in execution – the one promising spot seemed the table of students Iwanka had pointed out. When all else failed, there was youth. And here amid the going-to-flesh tiredness of the habitués of the café Leo's gaze came to rest.

Five or six were there gathered; a young man held forth. With strong bones and jawline, long hair and high spirits, he might have been someone Leo would have cultivated to manage a shopping-mall. Devil-may-care and life-of-the-party, he would burn out in a few years' time possibly, unless set on a responsible path. What Norman had seen in Leo that he himself lacked – greater youth and potential to pursue a business plan – Leo could now glimpse in this boy. And suppose he *were* to consider some business here, as the American had urged: mightn't it justify his errant trip?

Hating inefficiency and wasted time as he did, Leo was wondering if it didn't deserve a moment's recce when Iwanka said: 'You're not listening to me.'

He glanced to her. 'Sorry?'

'Would you like to talk to them? I told you I could arrange it. It might be more informative about our country than just sitting here not talking to me.'

Leo's eyes swivelled to take in the three or four girls the young man was holding forth to. They were attractive, yet less animated than their counterparts in London. It was a different world here, less sparky; and he began to intuit (where had the idea come from?) how a young man like this might be transfixed by a woman like Geraldine Scott.

Unexpected, unwelcome, this idea inspired an immediate fear: that the boy might be a version of the 'chauffeur' whom Twitch had told him that Geraldine was running amok with. Breathtakingly swiftly, male ire rose. And throwing back the dregs of his sicky vermouth, Leo grunted:

'OK, why not?'

So they moved.

•

When Krzysztof awoke, it seemed terribly hot. Above the trees, a haze covered the diamond of blue. Hardly any breeze spoke, but the murmurings that did made the evergreen needles seem to sway in answer, as if the fingers of a drowning woman waving farewell. – Not that Krzysztof had ever seen such a sight. Like many of his kind, he had only glimpsed the sea from an airplane, or on posters of Spain or such 'fun' Western places. Still, he felt as if he were in the deep blue now. Nor was it so different from being lost in the tall grasses of a Ukrainian rye field.

Something itched in his crotch. He felt all twisted up, as if his underpants had been put on backwards. Sliding upright against a birch trunk, he went dizzy again. His head pulsated; black spots returned, swarming like ants. Lord, it was hot here! Insects titivated – thick the mid-afternoon. He pulled out the elastic of his waistband and, yes, his underpants *had* been put on backwards. Bouncing up on one leg, he tried to rectify the situation but fell over instead.

When he came to, he rolled on his back in the leaves. The fingertips swayed; the murmurings seemed to say:

'Why bother, brother? You're only part of it now. Eat my berries and roots like some caveman or squirrel – like some painted bird out of one of those novels English lecturers teach, D. H. Lawrence and so on.'

He recalled summer nights in Pittsburgh, down by the river, where the low-life, non-university kids had revved their motorcycles and smoked pot, drank beer and listened to heavy-metal, growling through their stubble at their 'loose women' and fighting each other like wildcats at play. From far away on the opposite bank, middle-class kids had gazed out the windows of their parents' ranch-houses; they had longed to go wild too, but in their house-broken way it could never be quite the same.

Krzysztof sat.

Then there were the students at York University, where he'd gone on a shorter exchange. They'd tried to go wild as well, mocking at superficialities, porcupining away hurt with barbed cleverness. In secret, they'd longed for some outbreak of madness; but when it came, it was momentary, unreal, like Professor Scott's – a secret held down under the skirts, half pornographic, arbitrary and unrepeatable.

How his head ached!

Rolling in the dust, he felt bites on his thighs, tiny prickers in his chest. The sun pulsed on his buttocks and back. I want to stay like this forever, he thought, slithering like a snake or small beast through the foliage; like the gipsy-boy hunted across the Mazowian plain in that novel of Kościński's they'd taught at Pittsburgh... Wasn't Poland. Wasn't true. A haunted Jew's fantasy after the death-camps, written in Łódź during Communist times. Still, it was wild-making. And wouldn't it be fine just to live for survival, circling and perching, savaging like those rooks?

Wouldn't that be freedom really? a kind of panic? not mannerly Eng Lit conclaves nor quick screws in ex-Party hotels followed by a pretence that nothing had changed?

Students were sitting in the grasses before him, like at Pittsburgh during the spring. He'd been asked by the teacher to recite and was standing up despite the fact that he still had no clothes. To cover, he'd launched into 'The Second Coming' by Yeats. Musical, rhythmic, he was giving it to them with back-and-forth motions and arm-flexing gestures, until he became the falcon in the widening gyre, then the 'rough beast slouching towards Bethlehem to be born'.

The students, he knew, found his accent exotic. They were impressed too by how much better he knew their literature than they. So he socked it to 'em now in rock-star fashion: Mick Jagger, Jim Morrison. The only flaw to his act was that he had forgotten the last verse, or thought so. But glancing down at the book for prompting, he saw that there was no last verse, only the rough beast's arriving...

Krzysztof opened his eyes.

A wild boar was staring into them.

Timidly, like a curious domestic dog, it took a step backwards. As Krzysztof's pupils widened, it ducked its snout and sniffed through wide, flat, moist nostrils. He was transfixed.

Was he meant to be frightened? The boar's little tusks looked more grotesque than threatening. It seemed almost bashful, like a wizened old man caught embarrassed before having shaven off a tatty neck beard. Was this friend or foe, it seemed to ask.

Both stared.

Rising on an elbow, Krzysztof caused the beast to retreat more. Bobbing its snout, it took a pace further back, then stood perfectly still. More stares, impassive as hot afternoon.

Time ceased.

Something throbbing inside him, something he had never quite felt before: neither pain nor desire, discomfort nor unhappiness – was it fear? Yes, in a way, though it was more than that too. The throb felt triumphant, as if linked to some spirit that seemed to roll over all things: the pain in his head and bruises on his legs, the bites on his buttocks and shortness of breath, the seizures of muscle and nervous disorders, the twinges of anxiety brought on by the world, *his* world as he'd known it till then. A sensation of time flooding on, rolling forwards over these bright rye-fields, carried him with it, as if one with it now, no longer detached nor pathetically locked into his own individual consciousness. He was one of the pack, moving over vast plains, half-invisible within the long grasses as they bent in a breeze. Then a shot came, and all started to run.

In fact, there *had* been a shot in the distance. And pricking its ears up, the boar took off to the east.

Was this panic transferable? this instinctive urge to escape: to travel deeper into the forest, further and farther away?

Krzysztof was racing now between the leaves. The boar was much faster: it had vanished ahead; still he kept running, wild as a half-beast, hurtling onwards, or perhaps back in time. Then dizziness struck him. He spun like a shaman. O, if they could see him, the students! And that Englishwoman? Her eyes looming up, full of mothering pity, across this ocean of sensation – would he dance for her now? Pan? Dionysus? the mindless secret lover she had longed for in a dream, until the dream had scared her and been sucked back into her psyche, to be suppressed ruthlessly? But *he* would go on now. She who had set off this transformation could stop it no longer.

What were those silhouettes between the leaves? the teenagers returning, lured back by their fire, or the thrill of the monster who'd put it out? He would have to hide now: dive into a bush; go still as a leaf.

Through branches, he spied figures, heard voices, but here, like the boar, he wouldn't be found. And who were these shadows: these demons or giants or dwarfs?

As they came towards him, three of them walking, they couldn't see him, could they? – Whether or not, they were veering off now, striding towards a further field.

Actually, there was a road there – he could make out a low building: a roadhouse by a bus-stop. One of the figures, tall, dark, was holding a shotgun; then came a small woman, blonde, wearing glasses. She lagged behind talking; the third whom she talked to was Geraldine Scott.

Krzysztof tensed.

It was a long, leisurely gambol they seemed to be taking: a civilized, as if post-prandial stroll through balmy afternoon. From time to time, the half-paved track angled back towards where he was hiding and he could almost catch the sound of their chat – not the words so much as their music – and he recognized it.

The small blonde, pinched, unattractive, was the same who had talked about Eastern totalitarianism in Western drama at Kraków. Her voice, sharp and angular, had brought him out of reverie then. Now it wove around the subtler, stately tones of Professor Scott, like an oboe under the finer flights of a solo violin. The two seemed to go on as if in harmony.

Krzysztof shifted on his haunches to hear.

Along the edge of the wood he slipped, alert and committed. Only gradually did it dawn on him that he was naked still, covered in dirt, half-bandaged and, as it were, beyond the pale. If he leapt out to join them, the tall man might fire – he looked sufficiently weird. What to do then? wait? watch? simply see where they led her? Who *were* these folk anyway?

The man looked bizarre. A Chechen? A Kalmuk? Weren't many of them now in Poland. Having fought beside the Nazis, they had raped and savaged their way through too many peasant villages not to be as hated as the SS. So why would one be in the forest outside of Łódź? especially one dressed as a gentleman hunter in the style of would-be aristos who fancied themselves British lords?

Subtlely, Krzysztof was becoming a wild thing no longer. The boar's spirit had peaked and began to fall with the sun. His intellect was inching back up, as it were: as if it too were guided by an element – the orange moon, say, groaning over Russia to the east. Still, he was wary: the animal's sense had transfused itself into his consciousness to that extent.

The three veered off again, the road or track carrying them away to the west, out of the woods, silhouetted against the soughing grasses. The sun stood dead above Krzysztof's line of vision; it was about to descend heavily onto a copse of evergreens atop a far hill. In a hollow between this and where the three were strolling, the track disappeared in front of a low house.

Large, new yet not fully constructed (bricks and gravel stood by a cement-mixer in the drive), it looked not unlike one of those ranch-houses on the country club side of the river near Pittsburgh, or millionaires' villas in those photos of Spain. White-washed, rambling, with Romanesque arches and ochre tiles on the roofs, it lacked only a plush garden or patio to qualify as some palace in privileged style of the West; and Krzysztof wished he had binoculars to study it properly as the silhouettes became lost in its shadows.

Two or three dogs ran out from a carved wooden doorway; distant barks followed leapings around the Kalmuk. In a crescent of gravel where the track ended, a couple of Grand Hotel taxis were parked, second or third-hand Mercedeses either bought used or stolen from the West. Geraldine, hesitating, motioned towards one of these; the Kalmuk and blonde appeared to discourage her from whatever had come into her head. After a moment, they ushered her inside, but not before (so Krzysztof imagined) she had cast a glance back in his direction.

·

For the life of her, Geraldine couldn't remember the woman. (Her name was Gosia, short for Małgorzata, Margaret in Polish.) On the other hand, Gosia seemed to know all about her.

This had happened before in Geraldine's career – with students, at MLA conferences, etc. – so she selected one of her well-worn masks. Once more she was the brilliant lecturer from London, sometime novelist, semi-ambassadorial guest.

Gliding through fields with stately assurance, she struck a blue-stockinged balance between the neurotic onrush of a Queenie Leavis and the desultory contemplation of an Iris Murdoch. Thus she contrived to put out the requisite mix of self-confidence, idealism and zeal; of comfort in Nature married with civilized wit; of befriending in discourse, even amongst strangers, along with just a hint of remoteness – *de rigueur* among the English liberal classes to underline that intellectual humaneness must not be confused with an absence of steel.

Gosia was too full of herself to be taken in:

'We Easterners can't be categorized as one racial type any more than you Westerners can,' she said when the lady remarked on the exoticism of walking beside a Kalmuk. 'Communism or not, we have our divisions. Education, beauty, age, money – that's the big one now. It's not so different from you, only newer. The middle class – you saw them this morning at the Institute: Wanda, Gombrowicz, Spaliński – Solidarity or old CP, Pax or real Catholic, they're all a bit frightened, looking over their shoulders, and equally suppressive given a chance. That's why I quit. I was the best student in my year and went right on to become a lecturer. I'm still on payroll till the end of term, but I've had it. There're more exciting things to do – and more remunerative.'

They moved through an undulation of yellow grasses, nearly immobile under the heavy sun. Kirsan, the Kalmuk, now strode out in front, as if a Red Indian guide. It seemed like play-acting; no danger was more apparent than some rooks on the tarmac pecking at a baby sparrow which had fallen out of its nest. As the two women surfaced over a rise, these birds spread inky wings and, loath to fly off, skipped along the ground on their talons. Peering back out of predatory eyes, they made fine calculations as to when to return to their cannibal meal.

'They're frightened of changes,' Gosia went on. (Geraldine thought she sounded like a person trying to justify a rebellion gone too far.) 'They're alarmed at being poor and losing the respect the Intelligentsia used to have here. Some of them, like that old hypochondriac Weiczorek-Tatko, are worried about losing free health care and the value of their pensions; others, like that lazy snob Zakrzewska, are afraid of people of real merit coming up – the young, or those who don't pretend to be dispossessed countesses from Wilno. It's just as petty as careerists in the West battling for control; the difference is that we have this period of "transition" to live through. People like me dare to ask fundamental questions; so it's really churning. The narrow order those old time-servers moulded themselves to is under threat, even if we can't quite get rid of it. – I love living in 1990.'

Bony, diminutive, Germanic-looking, Gosia *sans* glasses might have been the spitting-image of Petra Kelly, late leader of the West German Green Party, whom Geraldine had once shared a platform with at another Council conference in the mid-1980s. Unlike a Green, though, this girl chain-smoked and ignored the abundance of nature all around. Something sickly in her, in the stringiness of hair and pallor of cheek – a kind of urban intellectual unwholesomeness – put Geraldine in mind of women around Trotsky or Brecht or anarchists like Danny Cohn-Bendit during *les événements* in Paris, 1968.

'Some of them were collaborators against their will. Spaliński claims that, after the War, with his family dead and home flattened, there was no option but to go along with the only power which could put the country back on its feet. He paid the price eventually: the non-Pax Catholics removed him from Deanship last year, and the Pope refused to receive his books among the gifts presented when he came to bless the Cathedral. Most of the others have paid nothing for their forty years of bossing around workers and peasants. For them it was as if the 18th century had never ended and they were still petty barons in little fiefdoms with an elected king. I'd say it was about time a real working-class hero rose up.'

'Lech Wałęsa?' our lady asked, half-engaged.

'Fucking CIA toad! As bad a truckler as that Gombrowicz you declined to have tea with.'

Geraldine just managed to keep from breaking stride. But if Gosia recognized her *faux pas*, she didn't let on:

'The real working-class hero doesn't truckle. He's a tough guy with tough friends, not boys in pink shorts from Harvard

Business School. He believes in being a man and does not take orders from lady prime ministers or eunuchs in purple skirts. He pays attention to material facts and doesn't want to be talked out of his fair share by some 'morality' grey middle-class weaklings rationalize to keep up their status. That's part of what's going on here. Another part is that the ugly – misshapen in mind as well as body – are looking for their pound of flesh. Then there're the young, whether ugly or not. They're always timid, confused and potentially angry, especially when they have no stake in things. Like the young everywhere, they're in love with cleverness, style, agility, colour, the anarchic life force – and death forces too. The West thinks they have them – a bit of rock music, keep 'em dancing late at night, taking drugs, making sex; try to make them believe that if they go wild against their parents and teachers, like in American films, they're "free". But the West is mistaken. There's something else here. Kirsan's got it; so do the Chetniks in Bosnia and Chechen mafia across the border. We're not the West and never will be. Our real revolution's only just begun.'

If she were in danger, there was nothing to do about it but keep on her mask and stay cool. An image of hostages in Lebanon came to mind: a CNN *aide-mémoire* that heroes were still needed even in a world dedicated to post-modern 'play'. But she was not dedicated to 'play', Geraldine protested inwardly. If individual self-gratification had been all she'd been after, she would have married Leo once he'd become a success and cheated on him as her colleagues did on their spouses. She would have left Krzysztof to be kicked in the street, or at least not come back after her morning's lecture to find him. She would have sent a note via Wanda and returned to Warsaw. Most of all, she would not have gone searching for help after he had leapt on her in the trees.

What had that been about anyway? Had he gone unhinged really? deranged by concussion? – There had been frightful bruises on his head: Wanda and she had taken an hour to bandage them. Was it possible that he'd been injured seriously? Somehow she doubted it. He was strong. Youth was strong, even in a deprived country. And he had been more than strong as a lover – memory of which now insinuated up through her as Gosia and Kirsan led on... She would miss that. She would miss him. It even felt for a moment as if she almost loved him, though she knew that couldn't be true. She no longer believed in love as an option, not between men and women, not like this. To say 'I love you' as Leo had so often to her was an obscure act of aggression; 'I want to colonise you' is what it meant.

No, she could not say that she loved Krzysztof. Surely, however, she was not proud of what she had done.

Shame swirled up now, like some disturbed genie – as if the sperm he'd pumped into her were suffusing her spirit to teach it a lesson in virtue. For the first time, Geraldine had an inkling of how the medieval mind could have come to regard sex as evil and develop the myth of the *Walpurgisnacht*. It was all terribly exciting when it happened, like sudden amnesia from the real world. But in its train came no end of phantasms, fears, monstrosities, beauties-turning-into-uglinesses and pain – like the boy's face battered and swathed in a shroud. I don't like sex, she concluded, hands deep in the pockets of her corduroy skirt; anyhow not sex of the kind she'd gone in for with him, like some half-demented creature in heat.

What had possessed her? What strange god or goddess had momentarily got control of this ordinary, rational human machine? Where had her unwicked gentleness gone? Would it come back now? Or had some wheel turned for ever, inside her, over him, almost around the world they traversed?

Half-blinded by the lowering sun and certainly dizzy from her incomparable day, she kept her eyes on the gravel and only emerged from her reverie to wonder if these two weren't leading her towards some kind of abyss. Of course it was just stress, fatigue and interpersonal paranoia; and from her years of climbing the academic ladder, she knew what to do. Still, it seemed like some ominous *deus ex machina* when an incongruous ranch-house materialized with a Grand Hotel taxi sitting outside of it. Equally, it seemed almost excessively portentous when Gosia remarked that the cab was not for hire and wouldn't she please like to cooperate and come in?

Alarmed as she was, Professor Scott made no sign of it. Doing as bid, she responded as if to just one more kind invitation to a foreign ambassadress in a strange, yet seductive new country.

*

Sitting among students in the Sukkierne café, Leo realized that he had no real idea of what Geraldine's life had been like conducting university seminars. His own progress as a property-developer hardly applied. The students among whom Iwanka had placed him were in their early twenties: old enough to have had live-in girl- or boyfriends, some even to have married. Their calculating functions had long since started to vie with their senses for control – not so much so as with the departmental secretary, but sufficiently that, even if he were old enough to be their father, Leo could see that he might be sized up as a prospective 'older man'.

Iwanka could see too; she didn't like it; already she'd become proprietary about him. Each time a student proffered a question, she inserted an answer as if their English were not clear, though in general it was better than hers – and than most native speakers'. This was vaguely amusing, if irritating. Leo could have put an end to it if he'd wished: the departmental secretary had no claim on him after all. But most of the students, who were neither dim nor unfamiliar with Iwanka's ways, soon communicated by eye that they knew what she was up to.

None of them, however, seemed to know about Professor Scott. One girl recalled her from the conference; but Geraldine's lecture had been among the first, and the University had not encouraged students to cut classes to attend until the last plenary session.

'That was fantastic!' the girl enthused, shifting focus. 'The speaker told us the future was all about Personal Desire.'

'No he didn't,' contradicted the young man who'd been holding forth when Leo had first eyed their table. 'He told us it was about finding some new Collective Idealism to Legitimate our Actions. I know: I read your notes.'

The others chuckled; the girl blushed; the young man winked roguishly. 'Mr Hooper didn't come here to listen to you argue,' Iwanka chided. 'He needs to know if you can help him find who he's looking for.'

All became sheepish. A dozen eyes peered at Leo.

'Arguing is what we do now in Poland,' the girl said.

'It's all right; I don't mind. It's interesting.'

He imagined that that was how Geraldine might have answered. But whereas she might have meant it, Leo himself was just playing to pretty faces and eyes. Ideas bored him: they could be channelled or suppressed as the energy they generated was used. If not, the person could be dispensed with – that was the capitalist way, wasn't it? Geraldine wouldn't have noticed the hair or the lips or the sexual promise threatening to absorb him here. How could a teacher operate on such a level, she used to say when he'd challenge her about it during their breakup. Had she been telling the truth then? Would it still be true now, or had she become a predator like him?

Pondering thus, Leo conversed with Magdalena, who was bright and perspicacious; Kasia, who glowed a bit less but was catty; Beata, who was quiet and round, exuding a nun's aura; Monika, who was punkish and lively, with make-up and spiked hair; Mikoi, who'd conjured a spectre of what his lady's lover might look like; Marcin, who played backup guitar, as it were, to whatever riff Mikoi was putting down; Andrzej, bespectacled, a bureaucrat in the making, who watched in silence and inwardly judged. Niceties passed. It was like being at a rather dull party in London: the kind that made him to look at his watch and, feeling trapped, make some offish remark.

But Leo was not trapped here. Proprietary though she was, Iwanka was hardly his date for the evening; nor were the students doing more than just hanging out. Probably they had nowhere else to go, he surmised. Looking around the rather sad café, he felt moved to buy them a round of drinks. Irritated though he was about wasting time (had to decide what to do next: leave Poland or find some new means of pursuit), he was happy enough to evoke their thanks. Each tried to pay. Grandly, he refused. 'What's six pounds?' he almost said before realizing that, translated into złotys, it might have been a great deal.

This idea spurred him to another bout of speculation about what it might be like to do business here. The thought was idle;

verbalizing it, however, allowed him to bask in yet more esteem – from all of them except Iwanka, who seemed annoyed that he'd got stuck at this table rather than exclusively with her.

'How do you find Poland?' punk-eyed Monika asked.

'I've only been here a few hours. Seems quite friendly. How do you "find" it?'

What struck him as polite chat the girl took as serious: she launched into a lament about how the place more or less closed at 9:00 p.m. and there was nowhere to go for a date as in London, nor any decent nightclub. Monika, it turned out, had worked in Clerkenwell one summer at a bar which Leo had helped put in business. This surprised him, but it was by no means unusual. Magdalena had the Council lecturer as boyfriend; he took her to Scotland once a year. Kasia worked each summer in Norway as a home-help; Marcin's mother had an export business to America in which he collaborated; Andrzej rode the bus to Amsterdam twice a month as a courier; and Mikoi went regularly to Switzerland on trips of uncertain purpose. An 'enterprise culture', in short, was already half in place.

'If that's the case,' said Leo, taking the bait, 'why don't you get some of these bright chaps together, pool your money, maybe even get a little more from a bank and set up a club of your own?'

It seemed so obvious that a hint of impatience tinged his tone, and six pairs of eyes dropped as if he'd told them to fuck off.

'That's the kind of small, fun enterprise that changed the face of Greece and Spain when I was your age – even Yugoslavia before it went bad. You get a sound system, set up a disco, buy a few crates of booze, get some lights, your friends to come – the right clientele – and you're away!'

Iwanka gazed at him with the pride of a mother attending a school presentation by her son.

'I'm afraid it's not so simple,' murmured Andrzej, suppressive.

'No bank would give us a loan,' explained Mikoi. (Unreasonable spite at the boy's looks had made Leo throw the bulk of the challenge at him.)

'I suppose we could try,' added Marcin, as if to mitigate the severity of the visitor's scowl.

'Of course you should try! It's what it's all about! You're out of Communism now. Do something to please these pretty girls.'

He was conscious of being a bully, conscious too of the note of Norman Niemenstein in his tone. And it was too easy: if he were really a good chap, he would offer to help them – it was his sort of business, at least not far off. But Leo was by habit a *provocateur*. And having provoked them, he now just sat back –

'Can't do this... Can't do that... It's all right for some... Maybe in the West, but not here, at least not yet...'

'Why not?' he demanded. 'You look for a space, get a lease, paint it the right colour, get the minimal furniture and you're away! Charge 10,000 złotys for the punters to walk in and twice your basic cost, maybe three times, for drink. You'll cover your outlay in six months, maybe less. Pure profit from then on!'

Only Marcin's eyes widened. But then Marcin was the follower of whatever male voice was most assertive. And now that his idol Mikoi had been cowed, Leo was the biggest bull, or bullshitter, around.

That's what Andrzej appeared to imply as he stated:

'You don't understand. Communism may be gone for the time being in Warsaw, but the little officials at the local level are still in place. What may be easy for Fiat and Nestlé isn't the same for nobodies like us. They can negotiate with the Ministry: if a deal goes bad, Western governments take notice, the World Bank makes a call, aid funds are delayed and they get their own back. But suppose we leased one of these shop-fronts in the Rynek, if we could afford to. If we got too successful, our rent would be doubled; the local tough guys or police or both would come round for a cut; some unemployed drunk would put a brick through our window because he was angry at the changes; everyone else would accuse us of being Jews and destroying the moral tone of the place.'

Embarrassed silence.

'I suppose it's not much worse than being in the Chicago of Al Capone,' spoke up Marcin hopefully.

'Or Glasgow or East End of London right now,' added Monika, embellishing upon her season in the West.

'And by the way, what is the alternative?' demanded Beata, surprising the others by putting her oar in. 'The boring career of teaching English language in one of our philological institutes?'

Twelve eyes darted towards the departmental secretary to see how she might react to this slur. Iwanka, however, was staring at Leo with a kind of parental glow.

'You see what you have done? You have started a small fire, an inspiration. I think you must remain and see that it burns smoothly. Otherwise it may flare out of control or die down and burn out again; and you wouldn't want that, would you?'

•

The rooks were squawking. It was early evening now. Above in the treetops, all species of birds seemed to have taken on a new life. They swooped and circled and sparred, called to one another across the fields, threatened small battles with enemy breeds, grouped and reconnoitred in various clumps, preparing to nest for the night.

Meanwhile, Krzysztof had given up his vigil. Now that Geraldine was inside that house, there was little to see, unless he verged close. One taxi had left, another arrived; the Kalmuk had come out and was sauntering back down the track they'd come in on; that was all. Any further idea of what was happening was up to him to imagine, unless he got brave.

About this, he was ambivalent. Here he was still naked in the woods, the one really free man in Poland, as he fantasized: for a moment yet the complete child of nature, as given over to impulse as the boar, no longer split between what was going on inside him and a mask worn for public consumption. He'd been a stage-Pole, charming, covering his real self in order to please; as such, he'd been made a fool of, beaten, stripped. So he would be that no longer. But what *would* he be?

Consciousness was returning to this extent. That in itself was a change. Wild and liberating as it had been to tear through the woods, it could not be a programme for life, nor even for long. As the sun fizzled, birds nested and temperature cooled, Krzysztof felt hunger surfacing over his horizon; but he was not about to grub for berries and mushrooms, the wrong ones of which could poison a city-boy. Daring as such things seemed on a page of a

Kościński novel, stalking wild rabbits and eating them raw was not a condition he aspired to.

Such atavism was not necessary anyhow. He was no gipsy-child hounded by peasants or Nazis: those days in Poland were gone! He had to find clothes now: that was the first step – a small tragedy for the spirit: the call of the wild was romantic; but there it was. He could hear Agnieszka, or his mother, chastising him as he trudged through the leaves. And what would they say when they *did* see him, his head gashed and bandaged? Well, that was tomorrow's bother, or the next day's. Now he had to dress, get to town and his car, then – *cholera!* (Oh shit! in Polish) Could the sequence of duty come back so quick?

Geraldine – he had to get her to safety, or at least come up with some story about where she had gone. She was the high-level guest still, Western visitor, friend of the Man from the Bank. If she were to vanish, it would be not only the Institute that would be furious: the Ministry of Education would be called in, maybe even the police, and then what? Even if this whole adventure had been her fault – even if all his trouble had been set in train by her – he had to make sure she was OK, or there would be no Agnieszka, no diploma, no job and no babies. He would have to become a wild boy forever: the one free man in Poland perhaps, but not free really any longer, because no longer by choice.

In the gloaming, he traipsed through the woods.

Freedom, he muttered: where had it got him? not quite as bad off as a drunk in a gutter (here was burnt-orange, gorgeous through the branches, and steely silver as the moon rose; there was bird-song, dying out softly, and a silence of twilight muffling cricket chirrups and barks of dogs far away); still, he was like a drunk in the foolishness of his situation – worse! A drunk could at least teeter down a curbside to shelter, whereas he still didn't have any clothes!

What had he gone in for? a bacchanalia for one, yet no one to consort with but shadows of demons and dwarfs. Now he wandered about aimless, helpless to find any sign of where he had come from. Vague recollections rose, such as of the monastery – might he not stumble on it? If so, what he would say to the monks? (It was not so difficult: he did look legitimately man-handled, didn't he?) Then the enwombing twilight was riven by voices. – The animal tensed.

Away to the east, north of a pocked moon, people were talking, or grunting, it seemed. Following the bird calls, their susurrations might have been the sounds of humanoids nesting. Slight thuds came, as of chairs being lifted, or items of baggage being hauled in for the night. Krzysztof envisioned gipsies or peasants who lived rough pitching camp.

Padding his way over twigs and dead leaves, he made out three rustic shacks: summer-houses meant for couples from town to stay in on the cheapest of state holidays. Moving in silence through deep indigo, he saw that it was not any middle-aged couple dousing their fire or folding deck-chairs, but the Kalmuk and one of the taxi-drivers from the Grand. Yes, there was just enough light to catch their features.

A cab had pulled up along the dirt track; its boot was open; they were transporting crates out of it. From time to time, one or the other would curse lowly; then came a thud on a floor, then footfalls cracking twigs back to the cab.

This ritual was performed six or seven times as Krzysztof watched; then the no-necked, burly driver got behind the wheel and, turning no light on, rolled down to the road. As he popped the clutch, the Kalmuk snapped a lock on the door of a shack and, picking up his rifle from where it lay by a birch, loped off, still dressed in that incongruous huntsman's gear.

Weaving slowly in and out of trees, he eventually emerged into moonlight, the animal following. The moon rose quickly now, spreading its shadows like monsters across trembling grass. The Kalmuk ambled relaxedly, as if out for a stroll again, post-prandial, only after supper this time. At last, he reached a light where the track ended in the paved road by the bus-stop and roadhouse. A dog barked, then whimpered; he went inside.

Krzysztof waited.

He could not follow to ask for help: he had no clothes still, and the dog was on guard. Besides, something was wrong here. The Kalmuk, the gun and the crates – what was in them, and why were they being stored in those shacks? Why weren't the shacks being used for their purpose, and how did this all relate to the house in the hollow where Geraldine was being – what? entertained? kept against her will? both?

Am I beginning to create some weird fiction out of my banged-up brain, he wondered. Is this some subtle revenge of circumstance: that, since *she* landed me here in naked, confused freedom, *I*'ve landed her there in thrall to unexplained people in a gangster villa (it could be no other in post-Communist Poland) with Łódź taxi scoundrels waiting in the drive and Kalmuks with shotguns on mystery treks through the trees?

What was happening here?

Padding back through the brush, Krzysztof peered into the windows of the shacks, discovered nothing. Trying the doors of all three, he found them all locked. He could unearth no clothes in this velveteen darkness; fruitless even to try. He had only these choices: to go to the roadhouse naked, watch-dog or not; to wait by the shacks and see what might happen; to return to the edge of the woods by the villa and try to get close enough to find out what was going on there.

Dogs were there too, of course; also Łódź taxi-mafiosi, possibly armed. The whole place could've been an arsenal for all he could tell; and what would he do turning up at the door, provided he got that far, dressed in only dirt and leaves?

It was as bad as the roadhouse as an option. And at least by the roadhouse there was a bus-stop, only one dog and no taxi-thugs; besides, it looked less like an armed camp – only the Kalmuk and whoever else inside. On the other hand, at the villa Geraldine would've already told them about the boy in the woods; so at the least he might represent no surprise.

Would that help? Would they let him in? If so, what? borrow clothes? take Geraldine in a taxi back to the Grand or the hostel at the edge of the woods, then back to Warsaw in the morning and everything happy-ever-after? It couldn't have been that easy. The animal instinct (or was it an overgrown boy's semi-conscious urge for adventure?) made Krzysztof certain that something more was afoot here. And as he crouched on his haunches trying to plot it out, another Mercedes sounded along the track.

A new taxi approached, possibly the old one returning. It

cruised ever-so-slowly, lights off, the Kalmuk preceding on foot. Krzysztof was closer now and, the moon being higher, he could easily see. The Kalmuk and driver transported five more crates, three from the boot, two from the back seat, each a yard long and foot deep. Thudding them on the same floor, they went through the same gruntings and lockings. The crates themselves showed no mark you could read at a distance; still, there was little doubt in Krzysztof's mind what they contained. Nor did it surprise him that on the outskirts of Łódź, or any depressed city in the new East, gangsters and Kalmuks should be up to this:

Traffic in guns. Or was it worse?

•

It would not be easy to say when Geraldine realized she was in trouble. There were small blips: Gosia's remark about her not having had tea with Gombrowicz; this funny business about the taxis not being for hire. There had been a hint of coercion in the way they'd ushered her into the house, and the look on the face of the host when she'd appeared in the sitting-room was for a moment quite cloudy. But once Gosia had explained who she was and why there, Vitaly Bazarov had smiled and extended a hand. Expressing delight that such a distinguished visitor from the West should have washed up on his shore, he invited her to sit on one of the wide, deep, perfectly vulgar sofas which guarded a heavy glass coffee-table in front of a gargantuan fireplace and despatched Gosia to make tea. Giving the Kalmuk an order in what Geraldine supposed to be Russian, he thus made both of her escorts vanish, as if elementals in some magic rite.

'I was hoping to use your phone,' she began.

'It would be of small use. The hospitals are too poor to send an ambulance these days, and the police would be unlikely to come for a thing such as you tell of. I have sent Kirsan. He will track your boy down. It will be better that way.'

Vitaly was round and balding. He had almond eyes too; also tiny ears and fine bones. Clearly a person of breeding, his hands were delicate, with nails so clean that they might have been manicured.

'Are you certain?' Geraldine insisted. 'I'd hate to put you to any trouble.'

'No trouble, no trouble. Kirsan will find him, unless the boy has become a creature of the forest and buried himself in a cave.'

It was not unlikely, given how Krzysztof had behaved. But this man could not have known that. There were those Grand Hotel taxis in front, of course; and recalling yesterday's contretemps, Geraldine wondered if a whole sector of Łódź might have heard about Krzysztof and her. If so, could word have travelled out here? But why would someone so evidently superior to the ruck round the Grand have been interested in such gossip?

Gosia resurfaced. Vitaly said something to her in Polish or Russian. She answered monosyllabically.

Nodding, he resumed to his guest:

'Since you are here, we hope you will stay to supper. By then perhaps Kirsan will have had success. In any case, it would be amusing for Małgorzata. You might even cast an eye over her thesis. She says she doesn't care if she completes it, but I say why not? What harm can it do to have the title "Professor", even if she ends up in import-export like me?'

'Vitaly has a degree in psychology from Moscow University,' Gosia stated.

'It is nothing,' he shrugged. 'So did Raisa Gorbachev, and look where she is now.'

The name-drop seemed far more innocuous than what passed over a London dinner-table. Meanwhile, the pouring of tea rendered the atmosphere so serene that Geraldine was moved just to sit back and wait for the leaves to settle to the bottom of her cup, Eastern-style. In this interval, she realized how worn out she was. Possibly because of it, she found herself imagining that these two – Vitaly so genial and Gosia so prickly, yet devoted to him – might be the perfect couple.

That entity had been so remote in her experience, and elusive in London, that she had long since repressed even a covert desire to be part of it. But here, perhaps because she could hardly keep her eyes open, the image evoked nostalgia.

'You must be shattered,' Vitaly murmured and, after a new word to Gosia – 'Perhaps you would like us to show you our guest room? Gorzata has been using it as a study, but there must be *some* extra space on the divan.'

Geraldine had sunk deeper into her cushions. The great stone fireplace behind her hosts' heads combined with the heavy wooden beams in the ceiling to make everything seem monumental, remote. She felt as if she were shrinking; being sucked into some Gothic castle in one of those sinister early black-and-white films. But such an idea was insulting. Suppressing it, she adopted a well-worn mask to reply:

'What a kind offer. Yes, I must be very poor company now.'

The pair murmured on in their mélange of accents while she finished her glass of tea. The sound of their voices, his mellifluous, hers softened, projected our lady yet deeper into her weird comfort zone. Like an uncertain moth, an idea flew forth that perhaps the perfect couple were a version of Lord and Lady Macbeth. As it drifted to the rafters, it was succeeded by a deliberate bucking up of confidence: they would look after her surely: they would find Krzysztof as promised – no use to suppose otherwise. She was in their power, a child trapped by its parents, for the time being without alternative.

This aperçu brought a curious feeling of liberation with it. Geraldine's world up till then had been made up of reason and will, of being pert and authoritative. But down in the darker parts of her psyche, she had not quite lost a chthonic urge to be overpowered one day... She recalled an ex-colleague, a youngish woman like herself, who'd gone in for vodka and drugs so violently that within six months she'd had a brain haemorrhage and nearly died. Now she was a vegetable living in West Wales, looked after by aged parents and entertaining herself with a cat, a TV and back-issues of *The London Review of Books*. Could anything be a more graphic warning of where the life of the mind might lead if taken too far?

Fear of this – of metamorphosis into something no longer quite human, a monster of reason and word – is what had led her into seducing Krzysztof. As her hosts murmured, she grew aware as she had after Kraków of how pleasing it might be to be caught in a language where one did not know a word. Here was a way-station towards respite from thought: like being impelled back to an era when all communication was carried on by grunts or gurgles and limited to the essentials.

For a flash she understood how Krzysztof must have felt when ripping off his clothes. It had only been half madness, the other half a quite proper desire to return to the primitive, a purely sensory language of body, eye, impulse and desire. How fine it might be to leave oneself for an instant, a day or a week! to leave one's conscious persona and become a creature of the trees. On the other hand, she was a woman, and English to boot. The forest was danger as well as an Arden. It was all very well, that sort of break-out in Shakespeare; but a sexual revolution now and then was all one could risk in this century post-Freud – as the Voice in Kraków had told them: those areas of culture which once belonged to the individual were now co-opted. And as Gosia rose and Vitaly ceased to murmur Slav words, Geraldine knew without question that she had to summon her public persona again.

'Would you like to come with me?' the girl asked.

'With pleasure. I *am* exhausted.'

Vitaly smiled benediction. 'Sleep well.'

'You've been very kind,' she replied in stateliest tones as the girl led her out into a dim corridor.

The ceiling dropped and passageway narrowed. Doors appeared with perhaps other people behind them: Geraldine felt presences, though none were visible. Half-light came from the forest as the corridor bent, passing a full-length window, and ended in a flight of stairs.

Down these they wound, to emerge in a hallway, off which further doors led. Vaguely she wondered why, if there were so many rooms, Vitaly had referred to only one for a guest, which had to double as a study. At this moment, however, she had no vigour to think. Besides, Gosia was now opening a door which led to a wide, low, rather wonderful wood-panelled den, an entire wall of which was plate-glass and faced a magical gloaming.

'Is this where you're writing your thesis?'

There were books and papers, bulletin boards pinned with clippings, an old typewriter, a new word-processor, pens, rubbers and other such paraphernalia. Evergreen needles tapped at the glazing; they enwombed the spot from all outer worlds. Here a thinker could think, though at that moment what impressed Geraldine more was that a sleeper could sleep.

Through the trees glinted a colourful light: Mediterranean, like she and Krzysztof had seen driving into town two nights before. Only here it was bluer, and cleaner, and drew her back from the life she'd been living towards some prevision glimpsed on the American road, or Italy in the '60s – a promise of other lands of more freedom, an invitation to travel, beckoning to Eastern European or beyond: some wilderness stretching to the mountains of the Caucasus or places yet more exotic.

These impressions half-formed. Without compass sense, Geraldine was hardly adept enough to map them out. Besides, as she lay down, she was entering a world more indistinct. Experiencing a kind of intoxication, though more of a drug- than drink-induced kind, she watched as Gosia whisked items off the divan to make space. It gave a glimpse on an alien mind.

From a board above gazed down articles in Polish and English: 'After Communism, Pessimism Holds On'; 'After Communism, Global Turmoil'; 'On Stop Lights, Chaos Theory and Eastern Europe'. From a board opposite stared out a photo of a good-looking man, Semitic, with sideboards: 'Alchemist At Large' stated a pink-orange sheet which any Londoner could recognize as the *Financial Times*.

Noting these subliminally, Geraldine also took in two fat volumes side by side on the desk: *Das Kapital* and *Mein Kampf*. And what could be made of this potent, unlikely mix, she wondered, dropping away. 'Intellectual Molotov cocktails,' she phrase-made to herself, then was into a dream...

She was lecturing in an old-style classroom like the one at the Łódź Institute. She was a character at last, a leading lady no longer. Little ticks, prejudices, signs of desire and frustration were shaping her words now, but she did not care. Glancing into a mirror, she grew conscious of lines, demarcations, cubes on her face which had not been apparent before. Should she be alarmed? 'But,' a better brain whispered, 'this is what can be so calming about middle-age, and why life begins at forty. You can simply *be* now, for years, until, happily, all begins to decay into caricature – like *Twitch!*'

Half-turning, she half-woke and recognized where she was. A sense of Gosia – she was a wild child as well, like Krzysztof, only streetwise, hard-carapaced, harbouring no thought but contempt for the timidities and second-ratenesses of the system, all systems: those Weiczorek-Tatkos and Zakrzewskas who made themselves out as victims yet at the same time enforced the orthodoxy of an antiquated régime. Spaliński was better: at least had created order here in the first place. But now came this new era: already it was decaying via Wanda, whose mothering Catholicism could only block free thought, and Gombrowicz, whose *Solidarność* credentials masked an agenda to get as many pamphlets printed by Western sponsors as he could.

'To the guillotine with them!' Saint Gosia cried to the stump-toothed extras in Geraldine's nightscape. Then came a storm: blood and rape in the streets as in Carlyle or Dickens. The petty antinomianism of those who sought changes inside the system was overwhelmed by the grand antinomianism of primitives on the outside. The taxi-drivers and peddlers from the market around the Palace of Kultur, the ex-hippy who had chiselled at the price of postcards, the no-necked waitress in the Grand, the drunks who had beaten up Krzysztof all rose up now. And Krzysztof himself led them, Gosia marching beside him, one of her breasts bared like 'Liberty Leading the People'.

Drum beats tapped: beats which led the *sans-culottes* to transform into legions of the Grand Armée. Tap, tap, tap. The beats slackened – a funeral march? Or was it the tap of a death march for the lady in corduroy skirts, back to vision, being led blind-folded up to the platform?

A guillotine blade rose. Geraldine's head twisted. Tap, tap, tap. Her neck stretched out, she looked up and saw through the gauze (it was cheap linen, riddled with holes) that Krzysztof, as if some wild man in woad, was rapping on the plate-glass at her.

Leo could hardly admit it to himself, but he had trouble recalling when he'd had so much fun. He hadn't set out to. Fun *per se* had never been his game. In his years with Geraldine, the things that had set them off from the crowd, they'd believed, had been love and work. Aesthetic pleasingness was as far as they'd got in the direction of 'fun'. And what was 'fun' anyhow? loud music? booze? parties where you could hardly hear yourself think?

None of these was exactly what Leo would experience on his evening in Kraków.

After provoking his table about the nightclub, he told them he had to get moving. What for, they asked; he muttered something about having to get back to London. What about his search for the lady lecturer, Iwanka challenged, less out of concern than to see if she could hold onto this prize catch.

'My guess is that that's useless,' Leo admitted, facetiously adding, 'She's probably half way to the war-zone in Bosnia by this stage.'

'We'll find her!' Marek volunteered, determined to keep up the spirits of the new lead man in the group.

'Sure,' seconded Mikoi. 'Let's cut to the chase. Where was she seen last?'

Giggling almost broke out. For a flash Leo wondered if they knew that she was behaving like a Donna Juana. To cover, he turned back to his theme of having to return to London, where-upon Iwanka observed that there were no flights from Kraków except on Fridays, he would have to go up to Warsaw and, unless he were to take a late night train, which might be dangerous for someone in an Armani suit and Church shoes, to say nothing of a platinum Rolex, he would have to wait until morning, though by that time it would be too late to catch the LOT flight till the next day.

'Are you telling me I can't leave Poland for thirty-six hours?'

The departmental secretary looked pleased. 'Would you like me to arrange a hotel for you? The Francuski is nice.'

'I'll stay at the Intercontinental,' Leo concluded morosely, remembering Norman Niemenstein's advice.

'You can't,' announced Andrzej.

'Why not?' Leo said.

'Because you're not a Jew.'

He stared.

'It's booked for the victims of Auschwitz this time every year. Closed to others for security reasons.'

Silence.

'Jews have too much power in our country,' Iwanka observed.

Andrzej looked a dagger at her. The others dropped heads.

'Ah,' Leo intoned, recalling Norman's tetchiness and trying to judge if Andrzej, so knowledgeable on the topic, might have been one of Poland's handful of remaining Jews. 'I guess it must be the Francuski then.'

Iwanka smiled as if he were a delinquent returning to mummy, who always knew better, thus should never have been questioned in the first place.

Mikoi clapped hands to dismiss any hint of bad vibes. 'Now that's settled, let's have a party!'

'Yeah!' hooted Marek Americanly.

Iwanka's smile faded. Reflective beams shone from the girls. They wanted to be noticed, Leo could see. They wanted to have 'fun'. And so they would...

They took him to the home of Kasia's elder sister, a thirty year old beautician recently split from her husband and living on the outskirts with her two children in a typical '60s pre-fab. The flat was high up: you had to climb seven storeys to get there. 'Lifts in Poland never work,' Magda confided to Leo as he began to feel like Norman in health as well as advancement of years.

Iwanka regarded the adventure as *infra dig* for a man of Leo's stature. She was sure 'Mr Hooper' (he'd introduced himself by then) would prefer to go to his hotel and prepare for his journey the next day. She made this journey sound like an excursion to the killing-fields of Bosnia itself. But everybody could see what Iwanka was up to by then. And no less than the others, Leo was content to wile away what was left of his evening in communal rather than one-on-one activities.

The sister's flat was kitted out with cheap, blond-wooden

cabinets like in a ski-holiday chalet. The kitchen was modern: he had seen worse in Southwark. The sitting-room had up-to-date cassette, video and TV systems. In a bedroom the children, aged six and three, played Lego on the floor just as their counterparts in London might have done at that hour. A fourth room was given over to the hostess's beauty paraphernalia, much of which seemed to be quite sophisticated.

Evidently proud to be conducting her own business, she handed Leo a card with 'Ewa' on it embossed in gold. Her hair was dyed black; she had an aerobic-enthusiast's shape and wore her make-up quite thick. 'She is not a good woman,' Iwanka whispered, adopting the tone of a 19th century missionary stepping into a brothel. Ewa saw, ignored and went to help her sister make canapés in the kitchen, several of which Leo gobbled down, having not eaten since the plane.

The others gravitated to the sitting-room and put on some old Beatles records. Leo at first felt quite patronizing about this: he had been part of the Beatles era after all, in the country which had originated it. (He had even once organized concessions for a six-day concert by the Rolling Stones.) But after a time, as fatigue reminded him of how far he'd come from that epoch, his air of superiority lessened. No one he knew could see him here, so there was no earthly reason, time being his own, why he couldn't just relax and enjoy.

Tins of beer arrived, wine, a flask of vodka, yet no one drank to excess. No one smoked either, except the hostess – although Leo caught sight of Mikoi, Marcin and Monika out on the balcony passing around something that might have been a joint. If it was, it was harmless, because they all came back in wreathed in smiles and ready to play games. These, it emerged, were so childishly amusing that Leo wondered if he had ever known normal fun at all in the competitive context of his Colchester youth.

There was a gentleness here inexplicably moving. Maybe he missed something in translation, but there seemed no agendas, except the transparent one of Iwanka's and something below the surface in Andrzej. But even they joined in as the others settled on the floor for a word-play in English, doubtless devised in his honour, called 'Fuzzy Duck'.

The object of this was to pass the phrase round a circle at such speed that the next person would get flummoxed and say 'Does he fuck?' – which terrible fate occurred first to Beata, who went beet-red; then to Iwanka, whose dignity hardly survived; at last to Leo himself, who laughed and became one of the kids.

Monika and Kasia took off his jacket; Ewa handed him a new beer. It was almost as if he *were* in a brothel, yet one free of vice. Magda unknotted his tie; the others cheered. Then Monika (she was clearly the lead girl, female equivalent to Mikoi) put a hat in the middle of the circle with pieces of paper in it, one of which was marked with an X. The object of this new game was for the person who pulled the X to become a 'murderer' and 'kill' everyone else with a wink, a fate which could only be averted if an unmurdered party called out the name of the culprit before being winked dead himself.

It was sometime during this game that Leo became truly entranced. Among other things he had disallowed himself in the years since Geraldine was a sensual locking of eyes, yet here the precise point was to stare into other gazes until you found one that blinked. The two girls who wore glasses, Beata and Ewa, dropped out of view quickly: the 'windows to their souls' were too dim. Mikoi and Marcin, covering excitement with giggles, squinted themselves out of sight; so too did Kasia, whose deep-shadowed orbs were very small. Magda, Monika and Iwanka, all of whom had large eyes set off with make-up, came to dominate Leo's attention entirely. At last there was Andrzej, who wore inscrutably thick lenses. He turned out to be the Murderer.

'It's not fair!' a voice complained, and the ones with the less stellar orbs flounced out to the kitchen, leaving Leo stuck to his seat and feeling drug-high.

The game finished (he would never have played at such a thing in London, but here he hardly wanted it to stop), the two young women of brightest eyes rose and started to dance. Too mature for this, or perhaps just annoyed by Leo's ensorcellment by her juniors, Iwanka followed the others out to the food.

As the girls stepped, he found replicated in motion what the eyes seemed to have promised. In their swirling and swaying, there was an attraction neither Eastern nor Western but universal. The music was Beatles still – he half-imagined himself in The Speakeasy or some other night spot of London circa '71 when he'd been their age and not yet in thrall to Geraldine Scott. The punky one, Monika, conjured a nameless hippy he'd met at a free concert in Hyde Park: barefoot and braless, she'd led him on a merry, LSD escapade from which he had almost never recovered. The other one, Magda, twisted a knee in so lithely, then rolled it back so suavely, that from his perspective of twenty years of adult sex he could hardly help but wonder what was transpiring between her lissome thighs.

Male magazine prurience threatened to take him over. This was not a condition not unknown in his life post-Geraldine; here, however, it half-alarmed him – possibly because the girls' come-on seemed so as if unconscious. Monika reached out an arm and tried to pull him up in a '50s-style jitterbug; when he demurred and tried to slope off to the kitchen, Magda forced him back with gyrating hands. When he protested he was too old to dance, both mocked him as 'Tata!'. And when he repeated he had to go find his hotel, the two of them declared: 'But we are going to stay up all night! The party's only just begun!'

Leoline Hooper had never thought of himself as a puritan. Why was it then that he felt compelled to evade their entice-ments? Because he was on Geraldine's turf and it might reflect on her? Because he feared the spell they were casting and could actually see himself staying in Poland and taking up with some penniless girl half his age? If he did such a thing, what would they say back in London? How could he dare *that*, instead of keeping on his well-known, half-respected rogue's progress among willing women of a certain age, who could never exorcize Saint Geraldine? Better to renounce, a voice inside him said; happiness is a butterfly that flies away. Better to exploit Iwanka if you need something: she's old enough and self-interested enough that an affair with her might constitute little more than one exploiter exploiting another.

With this idea in mind, he beat his retreat to the kitchen. Intending to say only thanks and good-night, he nonetheless hugged a vision of the departmental secretary offering herself as 'guide', a proposal he half-expected her to make. Quite an argument, however, was in train between her and Andrzej. And as he stood in the doorway looking non-plussed, Beata translated:

'Iwanka has said that Germans and Jews are surrounding Poland; they are already buying up Hungary and the Czech lands. Andrzej has said that that kind of talk is what keeps Western capital from investing here, and now Iwanka is saying that she is tired of Jews accusing the Polish people of being anti-Semitic – Jews don't have sufficient respect for the fact that Polish people let them have so many of the good things in this country before the War.'

The disputants' faces were strained; one of Iwanka's eyes seemed to have gone askew. Leo recalled a dinner in north London when he'd made some offhand remark, and Geraldine had snapped: 'With less than fifty years between us and the Shoah, I think it's in execrable taste for a non-Jew to even *think* a thing like that!' Silence had fallen. He had been mortified. 'History,' she had added, twisting in the knife, 'is a nightmare from which they're still trying to awake.'

Leo had avoided the topic ever since.

'I'm off now,' he stated.

Iwanka, perhaps mercifully, was too riled up to notice.

'Best goodbyes are the shortest,' he added, kissing Ewa on both cheeks (she offered a third, Polish style). Then he was out into the corridor and lift and before her door could re-open and some pixie or demon fly forth.

He pushed the button. Shuddering, the urine-scented compartment started to descend. Scraping gears as if stripped, it fell precipitously about a floor and a half, then hesitated before creaking on, making Leo recall Magdalena's words about Polish lifts. When it lurched again, nearly pulling his neck out of its socket, he pressed what appeared to be a 'stop' button, which worked instantly. Thus he became stuck between the fourth and fifth floors in a council estate on the outskirts of a city on the far side of a continent where he did not know word one of the language.

·

What is a Pole if not brave, Krzysztof thought. What is Polish history if not a saga of battles? And if many battles in recent centuries had been lost, it's how they were fought that mattered. No more rolling over for the powers of East or West! No more breast-beating and dithering, nor drawing pretty girls in a notebook! He had lost it: good riddance! No more lolling away hot afternoons in long grasses! He had done that: it was night now: he was hungry: the woman he was meant to be protecting was in trouble, it seemed; and something strange, perhaps evil, was afoot here in the woods.

He had pricks and scrapes and bruises. So? How had soldiers felt in the War, let alone Jews in the camps or gipsy-boys fleeing pogrom? – There were sounds in the leaf-mould, flitting shades as the moon rose, owl hoots, pulse of crickets, snap of twigs. Could the boar reappear, less friendly? Could something quite scary happen? Forget it, he thought. This was not an era of demons and dwarfs any longer, nor of witches and giants – let alone young men dressed in bandages, dirt and leaves.

Was he a spirit, Krzysztof wondered as he made his way from the shacks. Was he the modern equivalent of what had sent peasants fleeing in more antique times? *What was that in the treetop? live being? ghost?* Maybe all myths began with someone like him going a bit crazed and roving outside the pale, nipping in and out to play some prank or right some evident wrong.

There was that house again down in the hollow. Yellow glowed from its windows up across the field. Birds were asleep now, the sky indigo. Star-light grew bright here, free of town fug; the moon made the birch branches shimmer. Krzysztof felt his skin glint like scales as he crouched at the edge of the wood.

One taxi was gone, another still there. The Kalmuk was down at the roadhouse waiting for the first cab to come back.

The animal tensed.

Without thought, only action, he tore out over the field. Crouching again, he peered round at the moon arcing up through the trees. As if a burning, white eye of God, it spread his shadow before him over the soughing grasses, lighting a path. So he ran all the way now, down to the half-track which led to the door, then crouched in the brush a few feet from the second taxi.

All quiet here; sounds of night – that was all. No dog barked yet: maybe none had heard him. A half-breeze passed, just enough to carry his scent away to the east. What to do? creep around? peer into a window? rush the door like some full-blown lunatic, beating his chest like a monkey, roaring and raging as he got shot at or was torn to shreds by the dogs, wrestled down, captured? At least then he might be taken in and find out what had happened to Geraldine. But that would be an end to it: no job, no Agnieszka, no babies or real life; a mental hospital or worse – they might throw away the key.

Wild as he felt, Krzysztof had purpose now. His duty was to find her and get her home. If he couldn't, it hardly mattered what happened to him: he'd be in the shit anyway. If he could, it might mean not only fulfilling his duty but reaping real benefit. If she *were* in trouble, if there were something truly wrong here, might he not be able to turn shit to gold?

Rubbing more dirt into his body, he thought: the spoils to the victor, and victory to the brave. Then he set out for the wall of the house. No barks sounded here: where were those canines? Checking the wind, he slipped by where he would cast the least scent.

Crouching, he peered into a dark room; slipped on.

From the back of the house, a light shone into the forest. From a man's length from the building, it rose to the top of a protective hill to the north. Broad and long as from a picture window, it lured Krzysztof into the evergreens beyond.

Needles pricked at his calves, tickled the soles of his feet. Some distance into the gloom, he gazed back. Anyone who saw him could imagine his eyes merely those of some startled woodland beast.

Down there was a bedroom, a double-bed in it, a kind almost unknown in Poland. On this sat a man, round, slightly balding, almond-eyed, not Polish but Russian or Armenian maybe. He was talking, or in fact listening, to a phone. Beside him a table held a fax-machine, computer and globe of a kind found in antiquarian books about Faust. On the wall above was a map of Europe with red lines on it, one leading from Kaliningrad across the Baltic to Gdynia and down, one from the Caucasus across Ukraine to L'wów and Przemysl, one from near Bratislava up around Kraków. All of them converged on Łódź.

At the far side of the of bed was a second table, smaller, holding a lamp and a clock. Beyond this a second door opened, and in came the woman Krzysztof had seen walking with Geraldine. Throwing herself across the duvet, she kissed the man on his free ear; he brushed her off, the phonecall evidently being too important. Rising, she went to the window. Could she see? – But she wore glasses, quite thick ones. And meanwhile the man had put his hand over the receiver and said something to her, which made her look back shaking her head. Saying something more, he returned to the receiver. She went out.

After some interval, a second rectangle of light appeared thirty paces ahead. Like an animal alerted by noise from an unexpected direction, Krzysztof tensed, then approached this new patch. Halfway to it, a dog barked. The bark was low: more like a howl than sound of alarm. Blocked by the house, Krzysztof could not see the moon, though its light was tinting the tips of the trees; but from the sound of further howls in the distance, he guessed it must be high enough to stir all forest beasts and that the dog's bark meant only this. In any case, it quieted now to a whimper, then rose into a gentle moan.

The long side of the house extended perhaps a hundred yards beyond the light before disappearing into the woods. Creeping along it, he came to rest in the centre of the patch, well back from the window and too low to be seen.

The room in view here was smaller, with no grand bed in it, only a normal Eastern divan. No faxes or war-charts adorned its walls, only such materials as a researcher might need to help his or her task. On the divan lay a body, facing away. Its hair was blondish, its back slender, its hip high and covered in a corduroy skirt. Hovering above it, the girl from the other room appeared to be trying to decide whether it was breathing or not. At length, having apparently determined the former, she spread a blanket over the hip and, extinguishing all lights, exited.

The dog barked again – change of tone? The moon was higher still; general restlessness increased. Now was the moment, Krzysztof calculated: too risky to wait.

Creeping towards the window, he wondered if there was a door. Feeling his way along the glass (the dog barked again, not just moonstruck this time), he rose on his haunches and tapped.

The dog hesitated. He tapped again; the dog barked in answer. Having no time left, he tap-tapped until, ever-so-languidly, Geraldine Scott rolled onto her stomach and blinked.

It was a serpentine motion, distracted, almost as if drugged; and for a flash Krzysztof recalled some movement in a previous night. Then the dog's rage was upon him and, tapping a last time, he watched as her chin stretched and craned her face up and out, neck extended.

The eyes seemed to stare. He gestured at them – could *she* see? He couldn't say now – the dog barked inconsolably – had to get back into the trees.

Would he be discovered? Couldn't stop to assess. Cracking his way to the top of the hill, he saw the moon climbing higher and lighting the hollow below.

The dog had stopped raging. Krzysztof could make out its tethering-spot by what appeared to be a kitchen door. Growling desultorily, it loped around listening to other dogs under their own torment of moon. But this was poetry, not action. Had he succeeded in alerting Geraldine? Would it reassure her? What could she do now? He had to think for them both.

So he was off again, over the needles, through a sector of forest enwombing the house. Down the hill, across the track, into the grasses, over the field, he dove back into the woods from where he had lit out. Up by the shacks, he saw not a soul now. Along the track towards the roadhouse, he heard another dog growl, less alarming; and he crouched.

The door opened and out walked the Kalmuk. Lighting a cigarette, he sauntered into the road to gaze at the moon. The dog didn't follow; a car approached in the distance; the Kalmuk turned, expectant; taking the chance as given, Krzysztof broke from his cover, making footfalls as soundless as an Indian brave's. The Kalmuk tensed, sensing something behind him. Krzysztof leapt, throwing his arms around the man's neck, and squeezed with all his force until he'd brought him to the ground.

A struggle.

No time or consciousness to recognize any horror: in a situation like this, it was kill or be killed. He had no weapon: the man's rifle had gone down beneath them; it would've been useless at such range anyhow. There was no gag nor rope to bind the hands with, even if he had had the dexterity to do so. A moment's let-up and he might be thrown off and shot like a boar at the edge of the woods. So he gripped fast.

Vising the neck in a forearm, he almost passed out from the strain. But in the end, it was done. The beast stopped its thrashing. The killer stood and dragged his prey into the grass.

The Mercedes had meanwhile reached the roadhouse and was idling outside of it. As Krzysztof stripped the man's clothes, that absurd hunting gear, and dressed himself in them, a hoot sounded and a shadow traversed the light out of the roadhouse's door. A few words were spoken, quiet: a woman's voice. Placing the shotgun under an arm, Krzysztof stepped out and whistled softly in their direction.

The shadow pulled back out of the light. The Mercedes crept forwards. Krzysztof turned towards the forest and, with a slow, confident stride, led it up to the shacks in the trees.

III.

A Children's Crusade

> When the long winter nights come on and the wolves
> follow their meat into the lower valleys, he may be seen
> running at the head of the pack through the pale
> moonlight or glimmering borealis, leaping gigantic
> above his fellows, his great throat a-bellow as he sings a
> song of the younger world, which is the song of the pack.

> — Jack London, *The Call of the Wild*

She wished she could speak Polish. She wished she could speak Russian. She recalled going to a conference in Berlin one summer, a hot summer of breathless, fetid air like this year's promised to be. She'd fallen ill with the 'flu, and by the time she'd recuperated under the watchful eye of her feminist hostesses she could speak the language well enough to write a four-page letter to Leo in pidgin *Deutsch*. But she had always understood a fair bit of German, as a well-educated English person might. Polish and Russian were another matter. What passed between Vitaly and Gosia in the front seat was mysterious. And mystery provokes suspicion.

The perfect couple seemed to have had a row. When Geraldine asked one or two polite questions, such as where Kirsan was this morning and why hadn't they woken her up for dinner the previous night, the answers came out brusque. Gone was the genial manner over a glass of tea. On the other hand, it was early – only seven a.m. – and who could be expected to be chatty at this hour, even with the sun pouring as brilliant as torrents of gold across the shimmering fields?

'It's awfully kind of you to be taking me back so early,' she said from deep in the leather of the rear seats.

This Mercedes was a new model, and no taxi. Geraldine's idea was to be magisterial, kind. Refreshed after her nearly half-day of sleep, she was conscious again of her persona as novitiate *grande dame* and representative of the best of the West. It surprised her that Vitaly was too busy making stones spit from his tires to answer. And when Gosia turned and asked, 'Wouldn't you like to go on a small tour first?', she had her first glimpse of a long, winding road down into revolutionary melodramatics.

Like most sensible people when paranoia arises, our lady tried to sniff it back. Maybe they *did* only want to take her on a 'brief tour', though it was the last thing she wanted. But she could hardly refuse now. If they meant well, it would be unkind; if not, it might be dangerous. And what was her alternative anyhow? to fly out the window and hide in a neighbouring sunflower patch like Krzysztof?

The situation had not quite got that desperate, yet.

'Lovely,' she answered and simultaneously felt the previous morning's nausea come up. 'Did he find him?'

'Who find whom?'

'Kirsan. My friend in the woods?' – Waking and washing and getting into the car had all happened so quickly that she hadn't had a chance yet to ask.

'We are not sure,' Vitaly spoke up, speeding the car by the tombstone-shaped roadhouse. 'But we know he found someone. Measures have been taken. You must enjoy and relax.'

He said this without menace. But even someone suffering from more naïveté than Geraldine might have been put on alert.

'He means it,' Gosia added, less carefully. 'The best thing you can do now is pretend we're old friends. You know how to fake that: it's what you people get sent East for in the first place, no? to make out that you and I are just long-lost soulmates who've been exchanging ideas on culture like equals for years.'

They took the ring road around Łódź and veered off in the direction of Piotrków and Katowice. Geraldine knew there was no point in going on with chat: she was not going to be delivered back to her hosts, here or in Warsaw. She was some kind of host-age, though for what was unsure. Vitaly was up to no good with his 'import-export', thus the grim face and tough tone.

Thinking it through, she might have invented various explanations. At the moment, however, she was too fearful to do other than keep up her own cheery mask. When she spoke, the words came out as if sifted through migraine. Would she be beaten, raped, left by the side of the road? But they were civilized still, if kidnappers, weren't they?

After a spell, her fears began to settle. She'd been mastering stage-fright for years, after all; and via so many baptisms of fire, she should have been up to almost anything, shouldn't she? So her public persona told her. In support rose a troop of female icons such as she'd called on ever since having left dear Leoline. From George Eliot to the Warsaw *Nike*, they marched in to lend bulk and veneer. Underneath this, however, lurked weariness and these new, strange forebodings of breakdown.

Further beneath lay less familiar sensations; first the nausea, then a spectre of slipping down into some *Alice in Wonderland* psycho-dream. Against these, it was better to talk, she conclud-ed, even if respite from language was a thing she longed for. Then as they passed through the town of Pabianice, she had further inklings: of what would it be like to wander these roads, become like a child again, communicate by signs, concern herself only with living, surviving, begging for bus tickets, pilfering for food, grubbing for shelter when necessary.

Couldn't such an enforced simplicity correct something twisted up in her etiolated Western value-system? Couldn't she learn to refocus again on the small things, like drinking a cup of tea, having a cooked meal, washing her clothes, evading harassment, responding to genuine human kindnesses? Couldn't become her luxuries now? So she mused. And with her musing came two more hopeful thoughts: first, that she would be able to escape into some small town if need be; second, that she had longed for this sort of revolution in her life – which is what had prompted her madness with Krzysztof in the first place.

As these day-dreams swirled, Gosia continued to use the entrapment of the car to talk like a textbook at her:

'You will be interested to know where we are going. So I will tell you. We are going away from the way things have been. Vitaly is the future, and the future must move. We must leap from the past now, into the beyond. It is the present which is the enemy.'

'That is almost romantic,' our lady murmured. 'What did you say your thesis was on?'

'My thesis! That is just what I'm talking about. Gombrowicz is the type they promote these days. The other ladies of the Institute – your hostess Wanda – have made their way by not rocking the boat. You know what she wrote her *habilitacja* on? "The Higher Victorian Morality as Exhibited in the Novels of Mary Corelli". She took five years on it and two summer trips to London, sponsored by a European Community scheme. Do you think that's the sort of thing a real person ought to be doing in our period of history?'

Vitaly appeared bottled up in calculations. 'But don't you think it's worth at least finishing your degree since you've got this far?' Geraldine ventriloquized for him.

'It is worth nothing! Nothing in money – a full professor makes less than a petrol station attendant nowadays – and nothing in status – the life of the mind is the first thing to go once a dictatorship of the Intelligentsia falls.'

The two women glared at each other, one a picture of adolescent defiance carried into adulthood, the other of half-admiration. At least the girl's spirit wasn't mired in careerism, Geraldine thought, or fear of overreaching.

'Is that what the fall of Communism means?'

'Yes, in part.'

'But what about Havel in Czechoslovakia and some of these other new leaders? I thought they were all writers and philosophers. Don't they count as "Intelligentsia" too?'

'Yes. And there is Bielecki here, and Mazowiecki – tame dogs cultivated by your people and the CIA. Don't pretend to be shocked. We know you've been up to with these exchanges. Friendship has always been more than "friendship", even now. What about your meetings with the Man from the Bank?'

The girl swivelled forwards; Vitaly glanced at her, then at the rearview. His eyeballs were like onyx, Geraldine saw. So would the mask come down now and ruthlessness hidden behind it inch itself up out of a foreskin of politeness? It hardly mattered to them that her report to the Man from the World Bank was strictly to do with funding for higher education here: people devoted to intrigue will see only intrigue behind the unexplained.

'All right,' she answered, lowering her own mask a notch. 'If we're to be "friends" yet friendship is not what it seems, then why not tell me what you want out of me?'

She wouldn't ask how they knew about the Man from the Bank. As with the remark about lunch with Wanda or not having had tea with Gombrowicz, it was clear they had a network at work as in the old days. So was it back to the ambience of phone-taps? If so, how far would it go? electrodes to privates as in former times, or were these ex-Commies (as that's how she now defined them) yet more desperate?

'Just pretend,' the girl said.

'Pretend to what?' she snapped in a flare of defiance which, ironically, seemed to smoke out information.

'Kirsan has disappeared,' Vitaly spoke up. 'Someone may have got to our operation in Łódź. It's too dangerous to wait.'

'The time has come,' Gosia added, 'to act.'

Geraldine stared. Both pairs of eyes shifted, the almond ones of the Russian, the blue-greens of the defrocked academy girl.

'You're frightened of something!'

'Vitaly does not get frightened. Nor do I.'

'I wonder,' she mused, a sense of her powers returning, 'who's after you?'

Vitaly shrugged. 'Perhaps no one. Perhaps it was just accident. Perhaps it is even to do with your boy in the woods. In any case, Kirsan or not, we have no time for delay.'

'It's a sign,' Gosia stated.

'Sign of what? What *do* you want? And why don't you stop the car in the next town and put me on a train? I don't know what your game is; I won't tell a soul. I'll just make my report to the Man from the Bank, which has only to do with the state of Eng Lit studies here, and be on my way.'

'And what about that boy you were pleased to make your gigolo and leave behind in the woods?' Gosia challenged. 'Are you just going to walk away from that too? What if he'd been a woman? What about the ones left raped by Cossacks raging through peasant huts, or ghettoes during a pogrom? How would you have felt if you'd been one of them? Are you so concerned about your own safety now that you can't remember what brought you to our door in the first place? Does it occur to you that all our problems – your boyfriend's, ours, Kirsan's (if he has any anymore) – are a consequence of *you*?'

Her survival instinct returning, Geraldine knew now what her destination was: Wanda: that slow, steady simplicity, as in the rituals of making meals, raising children, running university departments in the face of uncertainty, chaos, change. To have faith was the secret. To carry on in an unstable world as if there were eternal verities still: that was the real heroism – not the outrage of Gosia and kind.

'So where *are* you taking me?' she repeated matter-of-factly as the Mercedes swept on into its phantom new world.

＊

Leoline Hooper was a changed man – so he wanted to think. To be caught for an hour in a rusty elevator in a suburb of a city where you did not know word one of the language was a kind of baptism by fire for him. It had been appalling to discover just how weak he was. He had yelled; he had wept; he had peed in his pants and slumped to the floor. 'Geraldine, Geraldine, why have you forsaken me?' he had whimpered with stupefying child-ishness. The naked lightbulb, the strange-looking words on the metal plate by the buttons – where had he been? purgatory? worse? Leo Hooper was not a religious man. Like most of his kind, the idea of religion seemed an irrelevance to him: a pastime or consolation for middle-aged women and womanly men alien-ated from the real life of the flesh and a bit vengeful or loopy as a result. But what was the point now? Where *did* it all end? He was not inspecting one of his developments in Docklands here;

he was not even safe in a hotel room like Norman Niemenstein. He was not in a concentration camp, true; merely stuck in a void, an empty space where no one hated or loved him, nor even knew where he was or cared.

And that was to be his fate now, wasn't it? Nobody to care. For nobody could care, the way he was going. How could they, attached to nothing but 'success' as he was? He cared for no one except a mirage of Geraldine; and she was just that, wasn't she? a mirage. His obsession with her was a function of his own narcissism. She was a convenience, a way of affirming he was too good for the others, the ones willing to care. And a few were willing, some even half-sincerely. Of course they had their self-interests, these Iwankas of his world; but what was any relationship at the start but a cabal of self-interest, and couldn't that become a beginning for love?... Love – what was love? If that's what he'd been pining for with Geraldine all these years, what did it add up to finally? Leo had always believed that she'd loved him truly, that she was the only one who ever had. But was it the case? How could she have loved him when at the same time she'd been so inconstant, so mercurial, so coolly obsessed with her own career? When he'd been unfaithful, she'd charged him with betrayal; yet who had been betraying whom? Who had loved and suffered the more? What had her focus on his infidelity been but a method of gaining the upper hand morally?

That's what it had been about in the end, Leo concluded now, stuck in the lift. Geraldine Scott had needed him to be unfaithful to her so she could be inconstant to him, yet sure that he'd stay like a dog at her feet. And that hadn't been love, had it? And though he had loved her, Leo had to face the fact finally that he'd been on a hiding to nowhere with her: that it had become an evil pursuit – a long and winding road down towards nemesis and the dark.

'Help!' he had cried out at intervals while ruminating thus. – It was like reading a newspaper while waiting for a traffic-jam to clear. From time to time you had to look up, honk your horn and move on a few inches; but really it might have been more practical just to turn off the engine and take a nap.

Cut the anxiety: that was the secret. Take it easy, and sooner or later something would come along. ('Help!') And sooner or later somebody did.

They heard him as they clattered down the stairwell. 'Help,' he repeated. It was 3:30 a.m. – an hour later actually: he'd not reset his watch from London.

One of the girls murmured something in Polish; the others ssshed; all pulled in their feet. 'Help!' he cried out a third time; 'I'm stuck in the lift!' And in a minute they were giggling on the floor above him, no more than a few inches over his head though separated as surely as by an iron curtain via mechanical breakdown.

'We'll save you,' called Magda.

'Don't panic,' said Mikoi.

'He won't panic,' chided Marcin in the tone of 'he's a *mensch*'.

Pull your socks up, thought Leo and, sniffing tears back, wondered how he was going to get the smell of piss out of his trousers.

'Beata's gone for the caretaker,' Andrzej announced.

'Tell her to get a move on. Smells like a doss-house in here.'

Someone chuckled. 'All these broken lifts are like that. Just like in Lewisham, where I lived.'

This was Monika. And from then on, the children kept throwing down scraps of banter, as if life-preservers to the man overboard. And by the time they had roused the caretaker and he'd come tinker with tools, Leo was back on dry land as it were. Persona re-erected, he could even preen himself to be fêted again by his liberating troupe...

There was six of them now, these merry wanderers: Magda, Monika, Beata, Mikoi, Marcin and Andrzej. Kasia, it emerged, had decided to stay over with her sister; Iwanka had apparently departed after Leo. How she had missed his cries when going down the stairs was a mystery, but maybe she hadn't. Maybe the Woman Scorned had decided to leave the scorner to stew in his juice, and maybe that would have been a just dessert. Oddly, however, Leo felt bereft by it. Though he'd only known her a few hours and found her intentions annoying, he knew where he stood with a woman like her. Out of self-interest if nothing else, she would be ready to mother him back to the full-blown shitness the world expected of him, and he rather fancied that now. Meanwhile, his newfound sense of ethical resolution told him that it was good for his character to pull socks up on his own. So he put on a brave, avuncular mask for these youths.

'Poor baby,' cooed Magda.

'We'll have to get you a new suit,' observed Monika.

'Let's get a taxi and get him to his hotel,' said Marcin.

'Where are we going to find a taxi at this hour?' Andrzej remonstrated.

'If worse comes to worst,' Mikoi mused, 'we could steal a car.'

'Or take the first tram,' Beata suggested, less impractically.

Yes, they were like weaving spirits out of a dream. And leading him out of his weird purgatory, they delivered him into a pink-purple dawn which recalled some drama of Shakespeare's he'd seen with Geraldine Scott at the open-air theatre in Regent's Park: one of those romances in which a comedic version of the Bard's evil-doers is jollied back up into normal good sense by the pranks of a sort of hippy troupe. Bundling him onto a tram, they even made him feel as if *he* might transform into a babbling, nonsensical teenager again: that adrift from the order of status in London, he might be able to slough his obsessional skin and in some incorporeal sense be reborn...

At the hotel, the Podroża (he avoided the Francuski, half-alarmed that temptation might be lying in wait there), he demanded the largest suite. A thick-set night-clerk seemed taken aback by the size of his group. But the 'Ballsack' rooms were available, so they went up.

Leo trailed behind an order for seven breakfasts.

'You are too generous!' said Magda.

'We'll help pay,' Monika admonished. (Mikoi and Marcin wore faintly predatory smirks.)

'What's money?' he shrugged and felt for once that he might become genuinely happy.

Untying his tie and unbuttoning his shirt, he threw himself on a sofa in the central room of the three which made up the suite.

'Make yourselves at home!' he gestured across an expanse of

thinning green carpet. 'Go to sleep if you're tired. And by the way, whichever of you chaps has a decent business-plan, now's the time to make your pitch.'

Was he conscious of winding them up? Could he see Marcin exchange a glance with Mikoi or Andrzej's expression go sour? Did he realize that he did not want to be a wind-up artist here anymore? some fat-cat from the West who doled out 'big willy talk', as Geraldine called it, then returned home to leave his listeners to feel slightly inadequate, or worse? Could he foresee that that was what was going to happen? Did he rationalize that, if they were going to succeed, they would have to put up with many wind-ups of this kind, as that's how capitalism worked? Could he tell that they had long since figured this out, being far from as naïve as businessmen fresh off planes from the West found it self-flattering to think?

'You don't have to reward us for getting you out of a lift,' Magda said. 'We'd have done that for anyone.'

'Well, nearly anyone,' Moni qualified.

'Maybe not Iwanka,' Marcin stipulated.

'Don't be uncharitable,' muttered Andrzej.

'I'm not rewarding,' Leo stated. 'I'm not pretending I'd join in. Even if I took an interest, Poland's not my patch; I only came here to find somebody. It just occurred to me that, while we sit here waiting for service in this unprivatized hotel, it might be something to chew over.'

Did he recognize that he sounded like Norman now? Did the unexploited potential of the place or apparent timidity of its people bring on a 'let's make a deal' attitude?

Coffee arrived, rolls: all the breakfast that could be scared up at 6:30 in the morning.

Taking up their cups politely, the children sipped as if at a formal tea-party.

'Maybe,' he continued, still playing *provocateur*, 'there's some place better than Kraków. A man on the plane mentioned somewhere called Woodge. Could use a shopping mall, he said.'

Mikoi, Marcin and Beata all clicked cups on saucers. 'Piotrkówska Street,' one murmured; a few words in Polish.

'That's a nice idea,' Andrzej elected to answer. 'But Łódź

116

would be even more difficult than here. In the first place, we don't come from there, so the locals would be resentful. In the second, it's the most unreconstructed Communist town in all Poland. Its trade was with Comecon and the Russians, so now it's really demoralized.'

Leo shrugged. 'The man on the plane referred to it as "the promised land".'

'It was once. For us Jews.'

Silence.

'Well,' Leo breathed, 'I guess I'll turn in. Maybe one of you'd like to be my guide up to Warsaw. I'll pay.'

'No need,' Magda murmured.

They seemed forlorn now. Maybe it was fatigue; more likely the ghosts of their country's sorrows passing over.

'You stay here if you want. There're beds in there and the sofas,' he added, going towards one of the bedrooms.

But he felt sad too all of a sudden – as if nostalgic before the fact at the dispersal of his little troupe.

'What about your girl?' Marcin spoke up.

'My "girl"?' – Were they going to ruin his impression of the virtue of Eastern youth by offering him one of these nymphs?

'The one you came here to find,' Mikoi clarified.

Geraldine a 'girl'? That was a laugh. It was exactly what she was not. There was hardly a hint of carefreeness about her: none of the blitheness that divided girlhood from the status of woman and made a man of his age long for his beloved as she once had been, at least in memory.

'Tell you what,' Mikoi went on. (He'd been watching with a shrewdness which justified Leo's first impression of him as a potential project-manager.) 'If we find her for you, will you back us in a club?'

Life was ironic. At the very moment when he'd broken his thraldom to her, they were offering it back.

'I'm not sure it matters,' he almost admitted, but the boy's look was so beseeching – all of theirs were – that it struck him that something for nothing was not what they were after. A bond was what they wanted: some genuine link that might be forged into permanent trust.

It was like love, Leo half-understood in that moment; and a wave of emotion surged to his throat. (Could they see?) It was just what he had *not* had with Geraldine in the end: a feeling he'd so longed for that he'd set out on this errant quest to find it and now missed all the more, sensing its evanescence.

'Well,' he half-stammered, 'If you're serious, give it a try. I still think it's better for me to go back to London. But if you succeed, I'll help you. So... get organizing!'

✳

Krzysztof no longer ran through the woods: he walked with deliberation – he had to. The taxi followed him to its destination by the shacks; he turned to help the driver unload the boot; when the man leaned in to pull out the first crate, he exercised the only option he had – to bash him in the back of the skull with the butt of the Kalmuk's shotgun.

All then went as if scripted for an American thriller. Sliding the slumped driver out of the way, he took out the crate; it was heavy. Vaguely able to read Cyrillic, he could just make out the words 'United Nations' on it. Not having a tool to pry off the lid, nor yet concerned with what was inside, he dragged it over to the door of the shack. Finding the keys in the Kalmuk's pocket, he undid the lock and dragged it in next to a dozen others like it.

Going back to the cab, he pulled out the driver and laid him inside by the crates, using the Kalmuk's jacket as a pillow, his neckerchief as a gag and his belt round the hands as a rope. Surveying his work, he snapped the lock shut and hid the key under the step. Returning to the taxi, he closed its boot, got into the driver's seat and started up. On second thought he got out again, went back to the shack, unlocked his way in and, leaning the gun by the wall, made another switch of mufti.

Dressing the driver up as the Kalmuk (the buttons bulged, but that made it easier to truss him up), he put himself into the taxi mafioso gear, then set out again. He felt sure this second change was necessary: the Kalmuk's English country gent's outfit would stand out a mile in Poland, and he was conspicuous enough as it was. A leather jacket and pleated trousers were perfectly credible, if these ones grossly too big; besides, the double change would leave a double mystery for whoever found the bodies.

Krzysztof hoped he hadn't hit the driver too hard. He wished the Kalmuk weren't dead. He could, if he let himself, imagine that a touch of evil had attached to him now; but he resolved not to think. To be a fugitive because he had to was not the same as to be a free man. It was to inhabit a stage beyond freedom, driven by necessity, unable to confide in a soul – some father-confessor maybe, but only in some distant city or country and only to move on once penance had been said.

And what was the point in such a confession? It only left you alone with a myth of Christ or Our Lady – hardly the same as being able to confide in a lover or friend... Agnieszka – he could not be wholly truthful to her again, not on an existential basis any more than a sexual one. He was alone with this accident and always would be. So was that what it meant to be free? to have blood on your hands through no premeditation of your own? to affect other lives for the worse when all you had wanted was good for yourself or somebody else?

How confused this new world was!... And he had been too hard on Geraldine. What had she wanted but to see Poland and give and take a little love, and what had been so wrong with that? Hardly worth the death of a man in the woods. But once things had started, what other choice did one have? Still, he wished he hadn't gone so far as to *kill* the Kalmuk... The feel of the man's neck still cracking under his arm – forget it, he thought: you have a job to do! His heart was not in this, however. He just wanted to get back to Warsaw, and rest.

How he wished for some friend to advise him! He was a loner now and always would be. He had known it for years but never felt it as a liability before. His mother had warned him; and it *was* what had landed him in the soup with Geraldine – gregarious young men who ran in packs didn't end up being prey to sex-seeking females. Which is why it was up to him now to set her free. And he felt sure that she needed setting free. Who could believe those 'United Nations' labels on those crates? Some Russian gangsterism was what was afoot here, and it would take more than just him to break her out of it...

Rattling the taxi over tram tracks of Łódź, he passed the old ghetto and Bałuty market. If he dumped it too close to the Grand, he might be seen by the other drivers; if he dumped it too far, one of them passing might smell a rat and set off a search for the missing colleague. If there really was a network of hoodlums at work here, word would get back to the villa where she was being held; and then what?

Krzysztof tried not to act as feverish as he felt. Pulling the cab up in front of the Centrum, he set off down a side-street across from Fabrycna Station to get back to his car. Passing the Cathedral plunged into darkness and most prestigious of Łódź textile shops, lit up as if on the Champs-Elysées, he saw mannequins in windows looking cool and chic. Avoiding their glazed eyes, he passed a solarium called 'Ewa'. On the sidewalk before it loitered two plastic females looking remarkably like mannequins themselves.

Tarted up in cosmetics and molls' versions of the jacket he was wearing, they eyed him curiously. 'Dziendobre?' one asked. The other smirked. His baggy clothes – did they recognize them? Had they seen him two nights before with Geraldine at the Grand? Were they trying to make out his features under the bandages, or did they just take him for some peasant in from Pabianice who couldn't afford or didn't have the sense to select trousers and jacket to fit?

Krzysztof hurried past. One of the tarts yelled – what was it? a price? There was a wad of banknotes, he felt, in the driver's pocket: that was lucky. But as he came up to where his Polski Fiat was parked, he realized that his keys weren't within a five miles' radius. – 'Cholera!' under his breath.

A hot flash of adrenalin turned him around and sent him back towards where he had come from. Flipping his collar up, he buried his cheeks in the jacket as if just one more no-necked, petty thief of the streets. The night breathed hot air; pollution filled his lungs, making him feel weak in the chest. He grew conscious of not having eaten.

'Coming back, hon?' one of the pair outside Ewa's asked.

Why was she speaking English all of a sudden, and why did it sound like a man's voice? – Krzysztof recalled black drag-queens outside the porn-shops by the depot in Pittsburgh.

'My dear Poland!' he muttered, 'have you come to this?'

When was the last train up to Warsaw? If he didn't make it, he could take a tram to the hostel by Łagiewniki Park, though his keys wouldn't be there either: they'd be in the woods in his tracksuit, and the caretaker would wonder why he was coming back alone, and if he stayed the night and went to look for them in the morning, someone would have discovered the Kalmuk already, or the driver or both, and he'd be right at the scene. For a second, he thought to look for the 'good witches' in their students' housing on Lumumba Street: an idea of their sweetness pushed him onto a tram up Narutowicza. But this took him right past the Centrum again, and across its plaza he could make out the taxi where he'd abandoned it. Two identical cabs had pulled up behind it; one of their drivers was trying its boot, the other using a pay-phone adjacent. More adrenalin rush, up the back of his neck. No time to be thinking of comforting young ladies now: a mafia network was at work here; Geraldine would be in worse jeopardy and he hunted down.

Get out of Łódź! his aching pate commanded. Get up to Warsaw and call in the cavalry!

That pate was muddled of course. What sort of cavalry did it think was on offer? A sense of his own survival impelled Krzysztof to half-run towards Fabrycna Station. This took him past the Centrum in view of the taxis, but the drivers were too buried to see. Taking no chances, he dove into the subway which led to the trains and let his half-run became full.

The gaggle of drunks that lived in the subterranean space muttered. He threw the leather jacket at them – hot as a horse-blanket now. A susurrus of weird imprecations faded as he emerged into the parking-lot by the platforms and slowed to a walk.

His heart raced. 01:19 read the digital clock over the tracks. Night was half-gone – how had that happened? He didn't look back as a taxi pulled up behind him – could've been normal:

taxis sat here waiting for fares all the time. Striding up a short flight of stairs, he passed confection and newspaper kiosks, shut, and got on the train idling at #2.

Skierniwice, the notice read – fine: he could change there for Warsaw. Letting himself into a toilet, he locked the door.

Voices along the platform, dark voices… Footfalls in the corridor, heavy footfalls… A whistle shrieked, a brake shunted, the train started its slow progress.

Was he safe?

Breath came more slowly. Tired, hungry, utterly done in, he unlatched the door and stepped into a darkened corridor.

Why were there no lights? But he couldn't worry about another thing now. The carriage was empty. He slumped onto a high, hard-backed seat and instantly slept.

When he woke up, the car was sitting dead-still in the middle of a forest. The moon ruled the world here: it blazed like a Klieg light around spectral branches of birch trees. Dead silence. Now and then a creak of the wheels or the couplings of the train, otherwise eerie stillness; not even a whisper of breeze.

Came an owl hoot, then a snore and a gurgle behind him. Krzysztof peered over the seat and saw an old man curled up in foetal position, which gave him a start. Rootling in his pocket, he found the wad of złotys: OK. The old man was no threat; if the hoodlums or taxi-boys had followed him onto the train at Fabrycna, they would have got out before it pulled away.

Nothing to do now but wait.

Keeping a grip on the money, he lay back. Listening to the old man's fustings and grunts, he wondered why the train didn't move. Dropping off a second time, he entered a dream…

He was naked once more, slipping in and out of the trees, the boar beside him. It could speak now, give directions, though he couldn't quite make out quite what they were. 'Speak up!' he cried as they ran through a phantasmal world, but it just kept mumbling and he struggling to keep up.

Then the lights were on and the train hurtling forwards. Clear of the woods now, it entered a preview of dawn, tinting yellow the hazy grey fields.

'Tickets, please.' – A conductor had materialized above them.

'Eh?' came a voice in south Slavic accent.

'Ticket, please.'

The old man did not have a ticket either, it emerged; and as the conductor wrote out his double-fare penalty, Krzysztof slipped the wad out of his pocket and found to his stupefaction that it was dollars, not złotys, and not just singles but perhaps forty or fifty one-hundreds.

'Ticket, please.' – Finished with the old man, the conductor was now upon him.

What to say? A hundred dollars might not be surprising from a Łódź taxi-driver – God knew what they got up to (was the bill counterfeit?) – but from a mere Polish student in ill-fitting clothes and with bandages around his head?

Cramming the wad back into his pocket, Krzysztof stated: 'I don't have the money, I'm sorry. I was beaten up and my money stolen, see. I have to get home to get more now, in Skierniwice.'

The conductor eyed him. A tense moment.

'Please,' Krzysztof begged. 'I *am* telling the truth.'

He could hardly give the facts now. To be detained even by a station-master at Skierniwice was not an option he could risk. He felt his muscles tighten, the legs readying to spring, the arms to repel the official or worse. Sick rose from his stomach – the Kalmuk: *why* had he done it? And would he be turned into a creature like this forever? some emanation of indeterminate, unwilling evil, racing from one fearful encounter to another, helpless to do anything but fight or flee?

He was on the verge of another breakout of the animal inside him when the old man wheezed:

'Conductor, he has no money? I will pay. I have these złotys that will do me no good in Bulgaria, where I go. He can repay me at Skierniwitz if there's time. I still have enough to get from Central Station in Warsaw to the Airport.'

Thus, for the moment, Krzysztof Robiński was reprieved.

＊

'It doesn't matter where we're taking you,' Gosia stated.

'I suppose not,' our lady lecturer mused, knowing she had little choice but to sit back and watch Central Poland pass. – There would be time for moralities later.

'What about, let's see – Bulgaria?'

'Why not?'

'They've got a new régime there; you'd like it. Their President is a shy, absent-minded, ex philosophy professor: the new, tame "Intelligentsia" your lot goes in for. Wants nothing more for his country than to sit like a begging dog at the door of NATO and the EEC. I say if that's where the revolution of 1989 has brought us, then it's time for a short, sharp counterstroke.'

'No doubt you would.'

'He's one of those incredibly simplistic intellectuals who's made his reputation by pretending that Communism was the same as fascism. A non-person under the old régime, he should be a non-person still. He has the old dictator under house arrest in his villa but refuses to liquidate him, or any of the rest of the old guard. How can you have a "revolution" without a blood-letting, I ask. None of them have read history.'

'History,' Geraldine recalled Krzysztof as quoting, 'is a nightmare from which I wish I could awake.'

'He doesn't have any balls. None of them do. In Rumania, Serbia, Russia, the old Commies still around – even in Poland. You know why?'

'Why?' our lady asked, though knowing she was going to be told inevitably.

'Because they're survivors. They're wily. They were the best and still are. And the people don't hate them. In their hearts, the people know that Marx was right, even if Marxism went off the rails. Instinctively, they realize that what has come is no better and may be much worse. Anyway, it's not for them – not for their health or their education or welfare, only for the capitalists of New York and London and Frankfurt who'll buy up our wealth in these rigged sales they call "privatizations", and the little gangsters and bureaucratic bribe-takers who are opportunistic enough to go along with it.'

'Maybe you're right.'

'Of course I'm right!'

'But I can't see how raging about it's going to help you achieve a better life,' Geraldine added coolly.

'What makes you think I'd care about that?'

'If you're not looking forward to a better life for at least someone, then what is the point of wasting your breath?'

'Because I'm angry!' the girl fumed.

'I can see that. So is all this just a ventilation of spleen?'

'Not quite.' – Gosia turned her face forward.

'I didn't think so,' Geraldine said; and the two of them fell into self-gathering silences.

What did Vitaly make of it? His eyes had stayed glued to the road. What did he think of his companion? Why was he with her? Gosia was not attractive in any visible aspect. Her spirit seemed too negative to be other than repellent. There was a kind of animal vitality to her, the kind one might find in a prostitute, drug addict or street person eaten up with AIDs or TB. An odd desperation seemed to hang about her, as of someone who didn't expect to live long. Everything was in the here and now: 'Eat, drink and be merry, for tomorrow…' But no. Despite riding in a Mercedes and living in a posh villa, she had no apparent instinct for luxury. Her passions were puritanical – such a rarity in this age! So was that the source of the attraction?

'I want the truth!' she demanded. 'And the truth is that throwing off Communism's only made for more speed, more ruthlessness and more crime. Teenagers imitate American videos full of violence; they maim each other with pellet-guns and hold up old men. People muster every złoty their family's been able to save by doing menial jobs in the West, or sending sob-stories to relatives in Canada, and start up shops selling cast-off Western goods that have long since passed their sell-by date. They try to pretend the stuff's better than what's made by the old state industries, because it comes in a glamorous package. They get gullible peasants to buy Wash-n-Go for a month, then everyone's hair falls out because you can't shampoo in the water here every day. The shops go bust and *liquidacja* gets written up on the windows. And then? social security? ha! a job in a state industry?

125

not with everyone already being laid off to cut "waste" to make them more attractive for Western carpetbaggers.'

'But how are you going to support yourself now, Gosia, since quitting the university?' – This was Geraldine's not-so-subtle way of trying to smoke out what Vitaly was up to.

She had an idea, of course: the Kalmuk, the villa, the girl's radical rant – they all added up to more than mere 'export-import'. But he was not going to just blurt it out, was he?

'What would *you* do if you found yourself living in a world spinning out of control?' the girl went on. 'Hang on like Wanda? Suck up to the West and the Church? But those wells run dry. They already have what they want here – don't need to buy us anymore. And without their grants and state funding, or any real knowledge of capitalist tradition except with the Jews before the War, we have to ride the chaos. What was immoral to us – capitalism, self-interest – is all we have now. So we grab what we can and sell to the highest bidder. And what can we grab? What do people, desperate people, always want throughout history?'

This was bringing it closer: too close perhaps. – Vitaly murmured something *sotto voce* to the girl. And Geraldine settled back into a rather sick sense of what was afoot.

'It's hard for everyone now: hard for the leaders and hard for the people. Some say that fortunes are easy to make, but that's a cruel fantasy. Anyone who appears to be making money is noticed as before; only now it isn't the remnants of the KGB or SB or UB who're after you, it's the mafia – or mafias, because there are more than one. The arms merchants, commodity smugglers, protection racketeers – all the underworld types you see in Hollywood films of the '30s are digging our graves now even as we speak.'

Geraldine studied Vitaly. It was hard to think of him as an aspirant Al Capone. How old was he? her age? younger? His nose finely shaped. The hair curled in tight little whorls behind the ears, suggesting exotic ancestry: Persian possibly. Well-dressed, with shirt pressed, there was something of the student about him: a kind of quiet respectfulness like she had glimpsed in Krzysztof. – But her tummy ached all of a sudden. Was she going to have her period?

'The leaders don't know what to do. Once they took their orders from Marx and Lenin; now they take them from Proctor and Gamble. But Western capitalists aren't committed. If the changes fail, they can write them off and move elsewhere: they don't have that much invested. Western governments aren't committed either. A "new world order"? ha! a "kinder, gentler" colonialism, half-hearted. Just enough presence from your Man from the Bank to try to establish a minimum system to make investment worthwhile. A collaboration between them and the few tame dogs – that's what we have. The natives can govern themselves or rip each other to shreds; it's not your affair.'

Now she was hungry. Were they going to stop? Actually, she was growing too nauseated to eat. Was she going to be car-sick? And if she got sick truly or had to go to the 'loo, would Vitaly let her? Where was the break-point between yesterday's civility and the new remorselessness in his eye?

'You Westerners are so grand. You come here so sure of your superior selves that you're half-blind to what's really going on. I've seen it often. All the young Americans and Brits who come to our Institute to get a little experience teaching so they can go back and get "proper" jobs in your universities – you'd think our students were heathen Africans of the 19th century, the way some of them talk. You know what you give us?'

Again, Geraldine knew she was going to be told whether she liked it or not.

'A mixture of power politics and economics at the top, moralism and lecturing in the middle and obliviousness at the bottom, where it counts.'

'I daresay you're right.'

'Of course I'm right! This is the way you've been handling it, or mishandling it, for centuries, in your superior smugness.'

'Handling what?'

'Your colonies.'

'Is that what Poland is now?'

'Not your exclusively, but the West's. And not just Poland – all the East. We're like the Western territories of America before they became states: when cowboys and horse-thieves and rough-justice roamed and Indians were massacred in a pre-Nazi version of what they call "ethnic cleansing".'

She could hardly mistake what she was up against: Lord and Lady Macbeth of a new Eastern kind. That was the basis of the girl's attraction for Vitaly: she got the man to 'screw his courage to the sticking place' and perform whatever chicanery was necessary in a disordered world. She kept him focused on the chaos, the breakdown of system, the unfairness swirling all around. Hers was a negative self-propagandizing. Without it he might've settled into what she'd described as the 'non-personage' of the President of Bulgaria, with whom he shared a philosophy degree. Vitaly could become a 'tame dog' or worse: an Oblomov, complacent, thickening at the waist, gently descending into passive self-interest – one could see at a glance.

Geraldine longed to detach herself into speculations: about men and women, the mechanisms of sex – all that novelistic sort of thing. Having ignored so much in favour of her career, she had only glimpsed bits – in her time with Leo, with Krzysztof even, their effect on her and hers on them. She had never stuck to a man long enough to chart the ups and downs of an overly-close *cloitre-à-deux*, let alone one operating in this sort of sphere; and it fascinated her. She longed to lay back and just let mum and dad carry on, observing all the little pressures between them, the secret weak places. But it was hardly the time for such study now. Her stomach told her this as much as her brain.

'Can we stop at some point? I'm afraid I must use the 'loo.'

Vitaly muttered to Gosia in Russian. It was as if he could not speak English at all anymore.

'We'll stop in Piotrków. He must use the phone.'

'Is it far?'

'You'll be able to wait.'

This was not an answer so much as an order, and Geraldine half-wished she could bring herself to retch all over the Mercedes's posh carpet and seats. But whatever she did now, she had to do gracefully. However desperate she felt, it wouldn't do to let on that she knew they were as bad as it seemed. And though it was clear she was being held against her will, wasn't it still far-fetched to imagine that they would subject her to *real* skulduggery? Kidnapped to Bulgaria? What on earth for? Why not Transylvania or Serbia or some war-torn province of the former Soviet Union – it made as much sense.

'Of course I can wait. You were saying?'

'Enjoying my little lecture, were you?'

'Rivetting. And your thesis must be quite unique too; I do wish I could read it.'

'Not likely. We won't be going back to Łódź for some time; not after what they find there.'

'You tantalise me.'

'I had the impression you thought you'd seen everything.'

'What are you into? money-laundering, drugs? I'm not up on these, though I'm sure I should be. I expect they've become the way of the world, and I'm just hopelessly old-fashioned.'

'You're just an Englishwoman,' Gosia sighed.

A surge of nausea, hunger and need for a loo made our lady snap, 'What's *that* supposed to mean?'

'That you pretend,' the girl shrugged.

'That *I* pretend? To what?'

'To be decent. As in Bosnia: humanitarian assistance, but no arms – that's your country's method, isn't it? But of course your private mercenaries make a killing on the side, as they always do. Meanwhile your soldiers are reduced to the status of being garbage-collectors of genocide.'

'Is Bosnia where we're going?'

Vitaly shot a new glance at the girl. 'Does he look like someone who gets involved in a war?' she returned, slipping a hand across the seat to massage his squat neck. 'Isn't it obvious he's made for more splendid things? Can't you just tell by gazing at him that we're off to a castle on the Danube and, if all goes well there, to see an associate in, say, Vienna or Zug?'

*

Leoline Hooper did not have trouble sleeping. In fact, it was the most pleasing rest he'd had in months. A blazing, bright morning seemed to emblazon his dreams, turning them multi-coloured. He was in Łódź, someone said. No, he was outside of that city, driving down to the sea. (Was Łódź near the sea? Did it matter?) Careening around tight lanes edged by greenery, as if the Cotswolds transposed to the Mediterranean, he espied in quaint valleys the roofs of old houses and new designer chalets tucked up cheek-by-jowl. It was a splendid, inventive exploitation of space, he reflected: architecturally and environmentally harmonious, yet visually modern at the same time.

Then he was walking down a street in north London: Islington or Camden Town. Turning a corner, he emerged into brilliance and saw Geraldine Scott stepping out of a café. Dressed in a long, clinging frock, she appeared, silhouetted, more narrow than he recalled. Her head seemed changed too, as if larger and cruder, especially around the jaw. She seemed coarsened in fact, though Leo told himself that on the inside she was kinder and more vulnerable than before.

Came a knock on the door.

'What do you want?' he barked before his mind had cleared, and Mikoi leading the others trooped in.

Beata laid Leo's trousers at the foot of the bed; magically, they had been cleaned and pressed. The group took up stations in a semi-circle around him, as if chamberlains in the court of some Jagiellonian king. Mikoi thereupon made a report on what they had done so far to locate his errant beloved:

'Magda has worked her British Council connection: as usual one hand of that organization doesn't know what the other is doing – they've lost track of your friend. Monika has discovered through her network that she was seen in Łódź: she gave a lecture there yesterday. Marcin has tried to get a hold of her driver in Warsaw; he seems not to have got back yet from the conference. Perhaps he is still with her, wherever she's gone.'

Leo twitched.

'Andrzej is on the road to Łódź already,' Mikoi continued, as if noticing nothing. 'He has a description of her driver's Polski Fiat: if he runs across it between here and there, you're in luck; if not, he'll find out what he can from his Solidarity chap at the Łódź Institute; if that fails, he'll carry on up to Warsaw. Beata has been trying to get through to the head of that same institute; she's a strong Catholic and would want to know where, when and how long your friend stayed and where she was now.'

'This is very thorough.'

'We hope you're impressed. We shall keep at it.'

The boy had a bureaucratic clip to his tone. None of the others showed any sign of fatigue despite having been up so many hours.

'We have not blown your cover,' Mikoi added. 'So far as our contacts know, we are only some group trying to publish a literature magazine which wants to interview Professor Scott before she leaves Poland.'

'We thought you might like that,' Magda averred, standing to the right of her leader.

'You think anything's wrong?' Leo queried.

'It is strange no one's heard from the driver,' observed Marcin. (Monika poked him in a rib.)

'We'll check that out in Warsaw,' Mikoi explained, half to disguise that they had digested all implications.

'In Warsaw? Are you taking me there?'

One or two faces smirked. In fact, these children had his number more than Leo would care to admit. There might have even been a touch of pranksterism to it as Mikoi explained:

'You can see that, if we're going to succeed, we're going to be quite busy. We have more phonecalls to make here and people to see there, which would only waste your time. So we decided that, since you know her already and we know she is willing, Iwanka might be the one.'

'That is,' Magda drawled, 'if you don't find her *too* tiresome.'

'Iwanka knows Warsaw and will be good as a guide,' Mikoi summed up. 'We've booked you into the Polonia Hotel for the night and will contact you there if we discover anything more before your plane leaves tomorrow.'

Leo stared at them in consternation. What alternative was there but to agree?

At the station in Kraków, he had a slight turn. He thought he saw Geraldine coming down a platform out of a train debouching from Częstochowa. It was another trick of the psyche, though unlike in his dream she appeared thick and peasant-like against the gauze-like light. Wearing a tunic and gipsy-style scarf, she recalled a woman he'd seen sweeping the floor at the University the day before. Only the eyes and forehead half-hidden gave him cause for a second take. But by the time he'd taken it, the lady had vanished.

Iwanka was decked out quite prettily this noontime. She looked attractive despite her late night. She had a small suitcase in hand but did not presume. In the compartment, she listened with half-comprehension to his tale of the lift, which had settled sufficiently to seem less traumatic to him. After he'd finished and was sitting back to gaze at the countryside, she worked to entertain him with a potted history of Poland.

She avoided the kind of outburst that had led to a row with Andrzej; still, she seemed unable not to lace her tale in strands of the national woe. Her parents had come from east of Warsaw, near Białystok, she said. Her mother's father, a small landowner, had been shot by the Nazis; so had her mother's first husband, who had been her father's best friend. After the '44 Rising, her father and his mother had been put into a work-camp; their house had been demolished; she'd had a stroke, and he'd had to carry her on his back as a refugee. Later, he'd only avoided being sent to a concentration camp because a Silesian countess operating as a hospital sister had certified him as unfit.

'In fact, he was perfectly able-bodied,' Iwanka disclosed.

Proof of this was that, after the War, he had married his friend's widow, taken on her two children and fathered three more healthy ones of his own. The last of these, evidently arriving quite late, had been Iwanka herself.

Leo attended this saga with intermittence. The way the woman moved all up to her own conception was faintly amusing. He was distracted, though, by that vision of Geraldine which had entered his psyche in Kraków; and in the day's third metamorphosis of her, he saw her now writhing in a hospital bed, hair wet and face strained, going through the last stages of labour.

Whose child was she giving birth to?

Iwanka had passed on to various subjects. Leo missed several as his eyes wandered over the greening fields. At last she returned to one that seemed obsessional for her:

'Like most Polish people, my parents did not like Jews. My father would say: "They kept to themselves here. They did not participate in the life of the country. They were always traders and cosmopolitans. They came to Poland after the Tsar drove them out of Russia and made every deal with us as if it might be their last one before Judgement Day."'

Norman now surfaced on Leo's inner screen. What courage it must have taken for him to return to this place! and for his people to have prospered here ever in the face of such prejudice.

'In the '30s, our state encouraged Jews to emigrate to Palestine. It is true that Polish people resented these outsiders, who had such power in industry and banking and trade, the legal profession and culture. The only parts of our life they were not dominant in were farming, the Church and the Army. We wanted to be rid of them, yes. But when the Germans actually *killed* them, we were shocked; and like most Polish people my parents felt sympathy. The Jews were our fellow-sufferers, and like many Polish people my parents did what they could to help them.'

This line seemed rehearsed, possibly even untrue. No doubt she had heard it from parents and teachers; probably she had recycled more than once for foreign guests. In the bright sun over the Mazowian lowlands, the tragedy it cloaked seemed as improbable to Leo as a concentration camp by the A303.

But there it was.

'After the War,' she concluded, 'the Jews who survived allied themselves with the Communists. Later they attached themselves to Solidarity, leaving the impression that they were opportunists. Now with the return of cosmopolitanism here, some of which is not very nice, Polish people wonder if the Jews are not behind this as well, as in old Party days. Polish Communism, you see, was started by a German Jew.'

'Really?'

'Yes. A woman: Róża Luksemburg.'

Leo let out a disgruntled sigh. 'Tell me,' he asked, 'how many Jews are there in Poland now?'

'Some say four thousand, others forty.'

'And how many before the War?'

'They say thirty percent of the population of the cities.'

'What a loss!'

'Yes maybe. On the other hand – '

'There is no other hand!' he snapped, cutting off the dreary subject for once and for all. 'Just look at the state of things. There's nothing been done of any value since then. You need them back and'll be bloody lucky to get 'em!'

Iwanka glared at him. 'I know that,' she stated. 'I was just trying to let you know something about how things once have been here.' Then with her weak eye shifting out of focus, she turned away and, rearranging the scarves over her shoulders, said nothing more for the rest of the trip.

Leo had discovered something about himself over the years: if no woman since Geraldine could mean much to him, then no irritation with any could sustain itself long. His crossness would dissolve and, by the time the female in question had reordered her mood and calculated her next move, he would have forgotten what the fuss was about. Thus on arriving in Warsaw, he was happy enough to let his guide re-assert command.

She would be going to the National Gallery, Iwanka announced, implying that there had always been a better reason for her journey than just to escort him; if he cared to join her, she wouldn't mind. Fair enough, he reflected, almost chuckling to himself. It was mid-afternoon now; and once he'd determined that there were no messages at the hotel, he was content to let the history lesson continue.

The Gallery was in a brown-grey, unkempt Modernist block down Jerusalem Street next to the old Party headquarters, which was now being refurbished as the new Warsaw stock exchange. The rooms were filled with 17th to early 20th century paintings, all derivative of contemporary works in the West. Monumental Romantics like Géricault passed. There was a special exhibit of some child-like Cubist stuff by a Pole who had lived in Paris and painted Picasso, though it did not look like him.

Everything struck Leo as quite second-rate, until they got to the basement and medieval galleries. There he had almost a revelation. He had never quite known how cruel the Christian imagination could be, at least in its early guises. The collection was of Silesian altar pieces; Silesia, having been German as much as Polish, had not been torched by the Nazis during the War; thus were preserved a great mass of carvings of kings and courtiers, all harbouring devils in the shape of monkeys or beasts, promulgating evil decrees.

Images of Christ crucified abounded, blood spurting from His wound and out of little holes all over His flesh. The spectacle was grotesque, sadistic, masochistic and revolting. And fleeing to Saint Geraldine in his mind, Leo could not help but murmur:

'No wonder they invented Mariolatry!'

'Please?'

He did not repeat it. Iwanka, perhaps proud of having produced a reaction, did not interrupt his gaze to re-ask.

That gaze was now transfixed by the crowning image of the collection: a huge wooden Pietà, quite pagan in its elemental force, in which the Mother cradled Her crucified Son, with triple droplets of blood oozing out in fine carving all over His agonized body. Compared to this, the epic Delacroix scenes in the previous rooms – colouristic celebrations of Polish horsemen trampling Teutonic knights – seemed positively civilized.

In some ways all was explained, Leo concluded. Meanwhile his cicerone, possibly embarrassed by the gruesomeness she had introduced him to, hurried them back out into the light.

They set off down Nowy Świat, 'the Champs-Elysées of Warsaw', though to Leo it looked rather more like the bare boulevard leading out of the centre of Munich towards the university and bohemian suburb of Schwabing. As Iwanka rearranged scarves in the reflections of shop-windows, he wondered whether the German city had ever seemed so down-at-heel, even after the War. As if in answer, or to contradict his impression that no colour could exist in this upper world, a freshly-done-up Greek café appeared around a corner, and she seated them in front of it.

Resting *sous-soleil*, they watched students pass through the university gates not far beyond. These young people, quite handsome, made Leo feel his usual evening's descent into missing Geraldine. Wanting companionship yet inveterately bored by whomever he was with, he would often cast round at this hour for some new face to stare at. A waitress half-returning his half-interested gaze made Iwanka rearrange her scarves again and whisk him out of there, saying:

'Ah! I almost forgot. We have hardly the time to get to Łazienki Park before sunset!'

She led him across the road to a bus-stop in front of a huge statue of Christ under His burden of cross. To one side stood a kiosk selling girlie magazines, also bus tickets, a packet of which she bought. To the other rose a domed building with a statue of Nicolas Copernicus in front, admiring which Leo was beginning to wonder again what one might do to bring life to this half-tortured place when a hand thrust him up into a vehicle that expelled a fizzle of farts and sped them back in the direction they'd come from.

Out of the windows late afternoon sun filtered gold through pale copper leaves. Along the sidewalk by a park, lovers strolled arm-in-arm; and Leo had to rejig his reactions again. There was a charm here, a civility even, quite lacking in London. Maybe it had to do with the procession of European faces unbroken by brown or black, or the sounds of the city unshattered by ghetto-blasters. (But you mustn't think that, a voice inside him chided as they stepped down in front of some ponderous government buildings. Mustn't let on anything that might encourage these people's essential racism!)

Iwanka led him across road again and into a square where a pretty garden had been carved out of a wood. High, budding trees enclosed the space on three sides; in its centre rose a massive statue of Chopin, his shadow draping over a reflecting-pool. The pool was ornamented by inactive fountains; on either side stood enormous black speakers; between them a young lady was playing piano. Though only 6:00 p.m., she was done up in an evening frock. From her fingers poured a medley of the national composer's most famous tunes.

Leo imagined this scene quintessentially Eastern. He couldn't conceive of a statue like it in London, though G. F. Watts's 'Force' in Kensington Gardens, which Geraldine rated, shared in some of its dark, monumental potency. Chopin grew out of a grand sweep of stone upwards; bifurcating from it was a gigantic bass clef, or perhaps arching phallus, which seemed to explode just above the noble head of wild hair. Or maybe the shape was meant to suggest a woman doing a dance of the veils, Leo mused on as the notes flooded forth, so passionate yet delicate at the same time. It was ambiguous. But then some mix of male conception with feminine achievement was how Geraldine might have described this music rippling over them in waves as evening fell softly above.

Late spring sun faded behind darkening leaves. Chromatic chords dissolved in dying half-falls, melancholic, heartbreaking, almost entirely at odds with the statue's deep-graven texture of menace. A Continental colour, Mediterranean in golds and blues, brought Leo's ex-beloved back for a fourth or fifth time – he had lost count by now. They were in Siena again, full of mutual hopes, life spreading before them like blissful dawn. But that was gone now – so gone! And in the midst of these old Polish couples in beiges and greys, a young woman who was ripe was waiting for him – so ripe, it seemed, that she was almost beyond it.

And what did *she* want, Leo was forced to wonder. Did she mean him to linger and let himself be drawn into some quiet, quaint existence like these old men with their brown-birdish wives? – But *what* was he thinking, a jealous voice hissed ('Geraldine!') as Iwanka sighed:

'Lovely, isn't it?'

What a cad he'd become! And yet, how could Leo Hooper, being who he was, fully resist? And so, draping an arm over the be-scarved shoulders, he pulled her closer to him.

✳

The old man, Dimitr, was on his way back to Sofia. He had come to Łódź to consult with a chemical factory which made materials used to manufacture munitions in his home town, Kazaniak, in Bulgaria. Dimitr worked for one of the largest defence contractors in the old Eastern bloc. He had done so for forty years – almost as long as the Warsaw Pact had existed. Since it had collapsed, things had become difficult: fraternal relations between nations were not what they had been; doing business across borders was no longer easy; currencies like the ruble were not believed in any more; old markets had vanished or become doubtful, such as Libya and Iraq. Where would it end, Dimitr fretted. Were it not for the conflict between Croats and Serbs, there would be no new trade for weapons in this part of the world. A surplus existed as it was, and Dimitr's company and home town were suffering as a result.

Krzysztof listened with half his attention. It was the litany of problems in every coffee-house since the fall of Communism; he just wanted to sleep, and to eat. But Dimitr went on. He was not a bad man, he protested. (Krzysztof could see this was so.) He had never cared for war and only done his job because it was well-paid. He had been lucky to have a good job; his family had prospered in consequence. He had a daughter in England and a son in Sofia at the University; the son was a professor and acquaintance of the new president. Dimitr believed in the New Europe, he said; but it would be a hard road to get there, and more blood would be shed before it was reached.

Krzysztof nodded. Did the old man notice the bandages and crusts of dried blood on his scalp? The surrealism of the situation almost amused him. Dimitr's chesty voice, with its near Russian accent, sounded like overdubbing in some antique Marxist film. 'We must move forward... It will be a struggle... More pain to come before the destination is reached...' But would Eastern Europe ever get to where it thought it was going? And where did it think it was going? Would it ever be defined in a way so it could be reached; or was it permanently ever-changing and, ever-changing, ever the same somehow, thus never to be arrived at?

Krzysztof shut his eyes. Ever, never, whither, whether, maybe, however – and before he knew it, the train had pulled up at Skierniwice. It was daybreak and Dimitr trying to make out the time on a clock above the platform opposite.

'My plane is at eight. Will I ever get there?' – He tugged at his bags in the overhead rack; the clock said twenty-before-six.

'Here,' Krzysztof offered and, against the old man's protests, pulled down both bags and led him out of the carriage, along the platform, up the stairs and across to a further platform, where the WARS Express from Berlin was about to depart.

'You are very kind,' Dimitr managed between wheezes. – Rushing to make the train seemed nearly to do him in.

'You've been kind to me,' Krzysztof answered, cutting a path through the streaks of sunrise.

'Forget the money you owe me,' the old man muttered. 'There won't be time for you to get it.'

'I'll help you to Warsaw.' – Krzysztof pushed him past a crowd and up into a carriage.

'It is not necessary!' he protested but was already wedged in, with Krzysztof climbing aboard behind.

The carriage was made up of sealed sleeping-quarters, the passage chock-a-block with people anxious to get to Warsaw early. Krzysztof nudged the old-timer beyond the 'loo door and crammed his bags between them just as the conductor came down the platform, blowing his whistle.

'You must get off while you can,' Dimitr murmured, but his words were drowned out by the train pulling away.

Krzysztof shut his eyes.

He would be a good Samaritan to this good Samaritan, he thought and fell asleep on the spot.

Held up between plump, tightly-packed bags and bodies, he felt strangely comforted. The train sped, slowed, stopped, sped and finally pulled into Warsaw Central at just past 7:00 a.m..

He helped Dimitr down and, carrying both bags, led him out to find a taxi. The old man continued protesting gratitude breathless and fretting about missing his plane. Sun blazed around the tip of the Palace of Kultur. Nostalgia for the Stalinist era, if not Stalin himself, could almost have gripped you, Krzysztof thought as he helped the relic into a cab. The simple necessities of that post-War era of rebuilding seemed to live on in a moment like this.

'Can you take it?' he asked the driver, offering a hundred dollar bill.

Without batting an eyelid, the driver slipped it into his wallet. Estimating the fare, he counted out 1,350,000 zł. in change, not taking the cigarette from his lips. You're in the capital city now, the look said.

Krzysztof gave back 50,000. 'Make sure he gets on the 8:00 a.m. flight to Sofia – Terminal 2. OK?'

The driver nodded. Dimitr cranked down a rear window:

'Thank you, my son. May God help you prosper in this crazy new world!' – Then like a mirage they were off.

A wave of emotion came up with the old's benediction. Maybe it had to do with the word 'son', or with the fact that he was too tired to think in any terms but emotional now.

Ambling in the taxi's wake, he put one foot in front of the other leadenly. Managing to get through the door of the Marriott's glass tower, he confronted reception.

'I must talk to the Man from the World Bank,' he said.

The woman at the desk did not raise her eyes. He repeated the phrase. 'Room number?' she asked.

Of course he didn't know.

She glanced up in response to his non-response.

'You must help,' he insisted. 'There's been an emergency' – by way of explaining his face. 'I must speak to the Man from the World Bank.'

'His name please?'

But Krzysztof did not know the name either. 'Just the Man from the Bank!' he said, the animal beginning to stir inside him.

'But there are many men from the World Bank here.'

'This one is responsible for education.'

'We don't know what they're responsible for. We only know who has booked the rooms and who pays.'

'But I must find him!' – His fingers and wrists recalled the person who had strangled a man less than a half-day before.

Shifting to diplomacy, he apologized and pleaded emergency again. 'If you could just wait over there, sir,' the woman concluded, 'I'll see if I can find someone to help.' And nodding to one of the leather sofas lined up against a mirrored wall, she gazed back at her computer-screen.

He might have sprawled on the thing and slept without problem. But alert to the need to keep the animal in check, he sat bolt upright and pretended to read the copy of yesterday's *Wall Street*

Journal which someone had left on the table before him.

From the railing of the *rez-de-chaussée* above, a man in blue uniform gazed into one of the mirrors inlaid into a marble pillar on the far side of a gargantuan chandelier. Unreal world here, Krzysztof reflected: decades removed from the so-called Grand Hotel in Łódź. Though he had lived in Warsaw all his life and sat in this lobby less than a week before, he felt a universe apart from the blue-and-white arrows indicating the way to a Bavarian businessmen's breakfast due to start at 8:30, or the early-risers in light suits and deal-makers of various ethnic groups who sat behind newspapers or milled about consulting expensive wrist-watches.

The two pretty Polish girls in fake finery sashayed through the revolving glass-door. A clipped British accent rose:

'I say, Charley, fancy meeting you here. Who's picking up the tab this time? the Know-All Fund?'

A pair of pin-stripes glanced at Krzysztof as they passed. 'Good lord,' the other accent trailed back, 'it's Lionel Barrymore in *Grand Hotel*! Think we should call the house-dick?'

In fact, that is exactly what the woman at the desk was doing. And before the animal could fight its way free, Krzysztof was being frog-marched out of there by two thick, well-manicured versions of Łódź taxi-drivers in midnight-blue uniforms.

Down Jerusalem Street beyond the moribund Soviet tourist agency was a long, low building with 'British Institute' in raised letters over the windows. He knew this place: students of English language throughout Poland were likely to have come to its library at one time or another, or applied to one of its many bureaucrats to go on exchange to a nearly mythical Great Britain. That was how he had once landed at York University for three months, though that experience seemed another world away too now: as if its safe Western environment, so green and calm, damp and cosy yet nerve-racked, had been a figment of a dream after a late night of study – of Shakespeare, say, alongside Kingsley Amis, as well as a monograph by Geraldine Scott.

At the door of the place, a small row was proceeding. A young man – sharp-nosed, apparently British – was trying to persuade a pair of Polish minders with beards to let him in:

'But I must speak to the English Language Officer,' he stated in remarkable Polish. 'I've just done a lecture in Łódź and been assured by Professor Scott, who visited for the Council there, that – if I talked to the E.L.O. before flying back to London – she'd back me to get a job that's going down there, with Council sponsorship, if you see what I mean. My flight is this afternoon: four o'clock, British Airways; can't be changed. So if I don't talk to him now, I'll lose my big chance.'

The young man wore a duffel-coat in spite of the heat, which even at 8:30 a.m. had become stifling. Handsome in the slightly feral way of the English, he had something shambling about him as well, as if the life-of-the-mind were too serious for one to look after one's appearance. Or maybe he was just poor, Krzysztof mused: there were many in England no better off than Poles, not least students, and just as discouraged about finding work. It would explain the cheap Russian bag which flopped on the pavement next to his down-at-heel shoes.

None of this impressed the Polish minders. Dressed in sharp suits and armed with mobile 'phones, one eyed the bag while the other explained that there had been a bomb-threat to all Western premises the previous morning and they had orders not to let anyone in except employees or those with firm appointments.

'But,' the young man protested, 'this is an emergency. I - '

It was an emergency only to him. Nor would any further recitation of his problem be likely to shift the minders, no matter how elegant his Polish.

Distantly, Krzysztof felt solidarity with this young man. But the scene made him realize two more things about himself: first, that there was no way, looking as he did, he was going to have a prayer of getting in to talk to anyone about Geraldine Scott; second, that his fantasy of returning from chaos to the 'real world' of a university job, Agnieszka, marriage and babies, being a decent chap and working his way up the ladder, was just that – a fantasy: a way of deceiving himself further. Because Professor Scott, having screwed him silly and ditched him, had actually offered to help this young countryman of hers get the very job that he had wanted!

So had she screwed *him* silly as well?

To hell with trying to 'save' her, Krzysztof concluded. And continuing on down Jerusalem Street, being eyed askance by this passer-by and that, he re-focused on the facts: he looked like a fugitive and was one now fully; the blood of the Kalmuk was on his hands and, if he didn't do something about it and himself quick, God knows what trouble he would be in – they would find the body in the woods (had they already?), the taxi-driver in the shack would be freed to tell his tale, the Polski Fiat by the Grand would be discovered, his clothes with the keys in them would turn up. So what had he been thinking of, imagining to save the day by 'calling in the cavalry', man from the World Bank or British Council? This wasn't an American western; they weren't a posse. It was Krzysztof Robiński who had to be saved here. To hell with the rest of the world!

'I would like a room please,' he said to the receptionist at the Polonia Hotel. 'I'm sorry for the way I look; there's been an accident.'

She eyed him curiously. Did she recognize the face? It seemed weeks since he'd been there with Geraldine. He brought his wad of złotys up on the counter as she pulled out forms.

'I have lost my identification card too,' he added; 'but you could look back. My name is Robiński. I stayed here a few days ago, with an Englishwoman, guest of… You must have a record.'

'Do you recall the room you stayed in?'

'462.'

'Did you lose something?'

Lose something? 'Yes!'

'What was it, sir?'

Geraldine's pearls!

'We have found the necklace and will be happy to return it if the lady would like to come in to pick it up.'

'She can't; she's gone, back to England. I could send it to her.'

'That's against our rule, I'm afraid. I shall ask the manager. Meanwhile – '

'Meanwhile, I want sleep, a bath, food. May I have the same room?'

'Please?'

'The room, I want the same room.'

'I'm sorry, it's booked.'

'By whom?'

'Please?'

'I mean: who has booked it? Have they arrived yet?'

The girl checked a ledger. 'They arrive from Kraków on the afternoon train.'

'Can't you change their booking and give it to me?'

'I'm sorry, sir – '

'I only need it for a few hours.' – He felt dizzy and crazed. 'I'll leave before they come. You could clean it again if they have to have *that* room. I'll pay.'

He pulled out a hundred. The receptionist eyed it, eyed his face again, glanced over to a colleague at the telephone switchboard; she gave a nod.

'I suppose it will be all right, Mr Robiński – if, as you say, you can be out by 3:30. But we will have to ask you to pay for the day in advance.'

He placed the $100 on top of the złotys. 'Do you have a lunch break?' he concluded, attempting a smile.

The receptionist, who was quite slim and attractive, answered, 'Please?'

'I just thought that if you or someone could go over to the Centrum and buy me a new suit, shoes, underwear, everything... My bag was stolen too, you see.'

'And the shirt off your back?' – She glanced again to the switchboard; the colleague rolled eyes. 'That must have made a pretty sight,' she said; and the two of them were left giggling like school-girl coquettes as Krzysztof went for the lift.

After a bath and some fiddle with bandages, he lay on Geraldine's one of the two pushed-together beds and slept for an hour. When he awoke, he was gazing at the Palace of Kultur through diaphanous curtains.

A slight breeze shook them. 'East!' it seemed to say.

Yes, he thought. Yes, that's where he would turn now. He had money; he had the taxi-driver's identity papers; he could merge with Russian peddlers on the train for Brzeszcz. Dressed well, he would not be checked closely at the border. But he must get away soon, the voice seemed to murmur. There was no telling who would be after him, or when.

For a time then he lay there pondering again on what the Kalmuk and others had been up to. What *had* been in those crates? At last came a knock on the door and, wrapping in a towel, he got up to let in the maid.

She gave him two packets, one of new clothes, the other with Geraldine's necklace in it. He tipped her in złotys, then gave her the taxi-driver's trousers, shirt and shoes to dispose of. Once dressed in his new suit – a standard, wide-lapelled, Moda Polska number in mauve – he lay down again and unwrapped the pearls.

Fingering them like a rosary, he drifted off. In his dream now the animal was setting out again across a swaying, shimmering, white-gold expanse of Ukrainian rye field. Through its smoke-like waves, he plunged and cavorted, until his consciousness dimmed and the world as he knew it was fading away.

✳

Was it possible that this was just some kind of initiation? Were Gosia and Vitaly just playing some prank to impress upon her the real nature of life in the East? It would have been nice. But the chances were slim. Anyhow, Geraldine Scott did not care so little for herself as to give these people the luxury of some figurative revenge on the West via her. She had to get out now. Whatever they were up to, she could not wait around to discover; the mask had come down enough. Accordingly, she let the upset in her tummy do its worst and, as they turned into the main street of Piotrków, retched all over the Mercedes' back seat.

'Dreadfully sorry!' and so on – she played the rôle to its hilt.

Cursing quietly, Vitaly pulled into a parking spot in front of a not-so-grand hotel. 'Get something to clean it with,' he muttered to Gosia, then leapt out as if the smell augured a bomb.

'Out!' the girl snapped at our lady in turn, yanking the door open. – All pretence to politeness was now fully gone.

Frog-marching Geraldine into the hotel, she asked for the women's loo. Passing Vitaly at a phone in a hall, they turned into a short flight of stairs. Gents was to one side at the bottom, Ladies to the other; between them stood a table for an attendant to sit at, though she was not there. It was clear it was a *she*: a closet was open with a smock, head-scarf and clog-espadrilles in it. Beside them waited a bucket, mop and broom.

Geraldine took these things in as Gosia pushed her downwards. On the last step, she bent over as if to retch again. 'Come on!' the girl hissed, trying to yank her into the Ladies', but our lady stumbled and fell to the floor.

'For Godsake,' the girl muttered.

'What is it?' Vitaly called into the well.

'Nothing,' went up the answer. 'She's more trouble than a child!' And Geraldine let herself be dragged into the loo, calculating all the while.

Once Gosia had stood her upright by a sink, she made her move. She hated violence of any kind, she believed, but *in extremis* what could one do? She was bigger than the girl; it was easy to get her head in a vise, a forearm covering the mouth. Naturally the teeth bit, and the pain was terrific – she wanted to cry out but knew she couldn't. She couldn't look back now nor hesitate; she had to squeeze with all her might, regardless of pain, till the girl went breathless (it couldn't take long, sickly as she was), then let up before she was asphyxiated. Too soon and Gosia might cry for help, too late and she might become a murderess; just right and she would be able to bind mouth and arms with a strip torn off her blouse – which is precisely what she did.

Easing the pressure, she let the half-conscious figure slump against a sink. It was gagging but still alive; if Vitaly heard, he would think it just more retching. Undressing the limpness, Geraldine trussed it up in a stall; her forearm was now bleeding profusely. Ripping a strip from the girl's skirt, she made a ragged tourniquet. Rifling her handbag, she extracted passport and money, then dumped the rest in the squirming creature's lap. Dressing in the smock, scarf and clog-espadrilles, she went upstairs, toting the bucket and mop.

This got her past Vitaly without him noticing. Beyond him, a corridor split in two directions, one back through the lobby, the other to God knew where. Geraldine took the second and, turning a corner, set down the bucket and mop. She carried on unobserved. Coming to a back door, she emerged into the street and hailed the first taxi she saw.

Did the driver think it odd that she acted out 'choo-choo' instead of saying a word? Whether or not, he delivered her to the station without comment, and she got into the first carriage of the sole train on either platform. Shutting herself into another 'loo inside the door, she prayed for imminent departure. With heavenly swiftness, Polish railways complied.

Trying to wash her forearm, she got no water from the tap. Leaving the 'loo, she found an empty compartment. Closing the curtain, she kicked off her clog-espadrilles and scrunched up on the seat. When the conductor arrived, she spoke no word in any language but sat up heavily and handed him a wad of złotys to take what was required. It was then that she learned that the train was heading for Kraków. It was the wrong direction, but that couldn't be helped. Once there, she would simply have to take the first train back to Warszawa.

When the conductor had gone, she scrunched up again and half fell into a dream. She slept through two towns where she might have changed trains and entered the French Revolution again; only now the image she saw as she stretched her neck on the block was not of a crowd of *sans-culottes* led by Gosia, but Krzysztof as if still smeared in woad knocking against plate-glass at her. She was in Gosia's study at Vitaly's villa, she realized, not splayed under a guillotine. He was slipping her out through a crack in the windows, and now they were running like wild things through a dark wood.

She began to feel sick; a branch hit her arm; evergreen needles bit into her skin. She didn't like it. She didn't want to be in a primitive world anymore, she protested, hurtling through strange spaces as if a hunted beast. She wanted to be clean now and for life to be ordered. She wanted to be with Leoline again in North London, with St Pancras Station on the horizon and the evening news flickering on TV. She wanted to be sitting on the sofa sewing a piece of tapestry when he got home; they would have supper; he would belch; she would fret about her day and mention a pain in her tummy; he would comfort her with automatic tenderness, as if her nanny as well as her man. Life would carry on as if they were a normal couple effortlessly making their way to becoming an old married pair.

Geraldine sat.

Was she quite awake? Without opening the curtain, she lay her head back (tortuous to find a comfortable position in these seats: they seemed designed to create a crick in the neck). Her arm ached. I will never leave England again for some royal progress as a lady lecturer, she resolved. I don't want pretentious 'adventures' anymore. I don't need to discover the leather jackets and thick necks, the demons and giants and dwarves, the visions of Second Worlds falling into Third ones, the graspings after First World-isms and descents into abysses of multi-coloured anarchy. I don't like the chameleons and con-men and hyper-conscious young women operating by a Nietzschean *Wille-zur-Macht*, the regions beyond good and evil or even residual belief in collective responsibility.

Catechizing thus, half in pain, half in dream, she changed trains at Kraków. That is, she wandered about on the platforms in a daze until she had stepped into the last carriage of the afternoon express to Warszawa. As it pulled out, her mind played her a trick. (Did yearning for England bring on hallucination?) There rushing for a carriage seemed to be Leo of all people. Arm-in-arm with one of his floozies, a Slavic version of herself a half-decade younger – her self as she had been before walking out on him – the vision made her think: if you gaze into your psyche too long, the monsters in its depths will stare back at you.

Is this the beginning of the true madness, she wondered more fearfully, laying her head against yet another torturous seat.

Landscapes slid past. They recalled Krzysztof and her seduction of, or self-seduction by, him. And why had she allowed that, she asked herself a last time – to penetrate 'the stories that haunt a culture'? to be penetrated by some novel inspiration? to tear loose from fate a virtually self-conceived child?

Circling back on this dumb, gestating suggestion, Geraldine

recognized that, yes: she had wanted to cause a splendid, irrational revolution in her life. She had longed to overthrow the orderly, intellectual régime she had so painstakingly built. At the same time, she had feared precisely what she had longed for, which was why she had behaved so half-underhandedly: as if to unwill what she had willed. That's how she had brought on this outbreak of madness, in him as in her. Yet, as Gosia had said, how could you have a revolution, even on a personal level, without at least some metaphoric blood-letting?

Rebinding her arm with the loo-attendant's scarf, she watched for Warsaw Central Station to arrive. It would be the last stage in her flight through this dystopic Wonderland before she could escape back to 'real' life and the upper world beyond. As the train wound into the city, the glass towers of Marriott and LOT buildings gleamed out their promise of the West, its relief and its ease. Never had capitalism's mirrored boxes seemed so comforting to her, so full of the sane and the good. The hypo-dermic of Stalin's Palace of Kultur seemed sinister by contrast: a superannuated reminder of evil times when people exterminated one another in the name of ideals. O ideals! she thought now. She was done with them forever! She would go find the Man from the World Bank, have him put her up in Americanized safety and fly home in the morning on the first plane!

Even as she resolved thus, the train slipped into its last tunnel; and vistas turned grey-black again. Hazy under fumes, the platforms looked desperate. Inured to abjection, a horde from Belarus, gipsies and exotic lookalikes of Kirsan, wandered about with floppy bags sausaged with cheap goods to sell. Some squatted on haunches in tight, watchful groups; others waited to pickpocket any traveller who looked as if he might have any spare cash. Through the smoke and the crush, hallucination rose again; and Geraldine imagined she saw the back of Leoline's skull going up an escalator in front of her, the Slavic version of her younger self still on his arm.

For a moment she chased it, if only to determine that it was no more than that: a trick of the mind. For an even briefer moment, she felt a wave of nostalgia for her ex-lover and what he had done in his own capital city of London, beautifying its decayed spaces and constructing shops to lift the sights of an English equivalent of these swarming unwashed. Then the wave subsided (it had been too quick to be fully conscious) and flare of Viking skull slipped out of view, as if the last vision of a knight errant who has suddenly drowned.

A glut of ex-Soviets trying to get down to the platform for Brzeszcz halted her progress. Struggling to push on, she grew nauseous, dizzy, and was forced to take refuge between a pillar and the wall. Once the crush had abated, she grew fretful again. It was as if she were seeing another apparition; only this time it was Krzysztof who came swirling before her, his skull bruised, though not swathed up as she'd seen it last. Yes, it *was* Krzysztof in the surge of the crowd; and a new wave of emotion, this time from her womb, made her want to cry out. – He *was* the father of the thing growing inside her after all, wasn't he?

O she was dizzy! And the head vanished, attached to a mauve suit so frightful in that sub-gangsterish, Eastern style that it could never have belonged to him. And he was back in Łódź anyway, wasn't he? Must have been found now and taken to hospital. Or had he pulled himself together, discovered the hostel again, slept for the night, picked up his car in the morning and got on the road looking for her? But Krzysztof Robiński didn't care for her really, did he? He'd only wanted to be rid of her in the end. And how could she have blamed him?

He had a life to lead, this sweet lad with a future – more so than she did perhaps. Geraldine hoped he was all right but felt sure he would be better off without her. And she didn't love him either: it had only been what it was. Besides, the last thing a woman in her position needed, if there were actually something growing inside her – if this was not just some hormonally-superannuated female's mad dream – was some dependent Eastern European youth traipsing to the West to play Joseph to its immaculate conception.

Have to be on your own now, she chastised herself, reverting to a form she had used in the years since fleeing faithless Leoline. 'Pull your socks up!' she mouthed in the phrase of some generalized British nanny. And as the crush funnelled its way down the escalator for Brzeszcz, she fought her way up through a last wave of petty traders into the crystalline elegance and flat retreat of the 'American Palace of Culture'.

✳

Long summer evenings are glorious throughout northern Europe, but this one struck Leo as more memorable than many he had known in London or Berlin. The pastorale of Łazienki Park had prepared him almost to give up. The gilded pastels of the Old Town Square quickened his tendency to want just to drift. The square itself brought to mind Siena, where he travelled again with Geraldine Scott.

Iwanka did not interrupt his precious reveries. Maybe she was indulging in some Mediterranean fantasy of her own as they sat in an open-air café nursing a drink. A Latin American band played pipe-and-drum music. She found it romantic, she said. When it had finished and the hat was passed, she bought a tape of its songs with her hard-earned złotys to give Leo, 'as a souvenir of our day together in Warsaw'.

Feeling sentimental, he was moved to say, 'How would you like me to take you to the best restaurant this town has to offer?' So as the light faded, they crossed to a beamed cavern, which looked something like a Bavarian beer-*stube*, only smaller and roughly French. Copper pans hung on a rear wall by the kitchen. The main room faced outwards onto the square, where the light now withdrew to the highest windows, turning them bronze.

The sky above deepened to indigo as they studied their menus. Leo decided on caviar blinis to begin with, a treat Iwanka seldom had had. She communicated her appreciation by a new decorum, even sweetness. At this early hour, they had the place to themselves. And with the vodka and red wine (the only good French wine in Warsaw, the waiter maintained), Leo grew calmly forgetful – indeed almost *there*.

Geraldine's shadow passed; he entered the moment; he even began to wonder if he might become permanently happy again. A short list of features in his new companion actually pleased him: the eyes which were pretty when not pulled askew by stress;

the skin which was peach-like; the nose finely shaped and lips which were full, if somewhat too reddened by gloss. Details hardly mattered. What was important was that she was keen to please him and he apparently able to please her.

However rare in her case, a treat like this set Leo back less than a business lunch in Docklands. And it was fun to entertain someone so deprived – even more so when that someone had looks, a capacity to charm and attitudes which might be readjusted in time without too much anguish.

Iwanka, of course, was not the sole object of Leo's patronizing attentions. Studying the place, he estimated that – if this were the best the capital city had to offer – the potential for development here was truly immense. As food came and plates went, he found himself wanting to get back to London less and less. He even began to fantasize a future in some new world like this, perhaps with some female like her on his arm.

Drifting thus, he hardly noticed a table nearby filling with American couples. Dark-suited, thirty-odd, they doubtless emanated from the embassy or some multinational 'org'.

'I don't care how much it costs,' one of the women brayed. 'I just need an edible meal for a change.'

'I heard another story today,' said one of the men, 'about a guy not being able to handle it in the East – Fulbright lecturer, the new one they sent to Katowice last winter: God knows how anyone survives in that air. 'parently he started with high hopes, then slid into the charcoal-grey depression we all learn to know an' love here. Began to think his Polish colleagues were conspiring against him – sabotaging his hot water supply, things like that. He complained to Warsaw, got the usual inaction. Then before anyone'd noticed the danger signals, he'd barricaded himself in his grim little university apartment, with the walls seeping sick-building syndrome and trams clanging back and forth outside so's he could only sleep from midnight till three in the morning. Feel awful sorry for the poor fucker. After a month, he had to be invalided back to Milwaukee.'

'It's all down to pollution,' a second man opined. 'A Peace Corps expert told me that the symptoms of lead-poisoning are loss of short-term memory, inhibited motor movements, reduced intellectual powers and bone damage.'

'I've got all four!' joked the first.

'Damage to your bone too?' quipped the other.

'Nah,' a second woman brayed saucily. 'Eddie's too much of a horn-dawg for that. And a good woman always has a cure for it.'

They laughed.

The atmosphere broken, Leo said to his guest: 'Shall we get the bill?'

'Rachunek,' she corrected.

'Sorry?'

'Rachunek, it means "bill" in Polish. Just try. If you don't learn at least one word in our language, I will have been a complete failure.'

'Ah,' he answered; then with a Don Juan's caress – 'So: what is the Polish for "love"?'

Leo Hooper had a lyrical side to him. Had that been a reason for his failure with Geraldine Scott? She had been verbal, he not. Silence appealed to him, sensual pleasures, sights – all of which were present, like a promise of calm, dreamless nights, as he led Iwanka back towards the hotel.

The spire of the Palace of Kultur guided their steps. They passed the Warsaw *Nike*, the Great Theatre, the War Memorial, several government buildings and the Russian market spread out on a vast central square. Every new vista conjured a brainstorm for Leo. Flashes of innovations he'd introduced from Covent Garden to Camden Lock imposed themselves on his inner screen. And if Warsaw were all 'sewn up' as Norman had maintained, then why not take a tip and try this other place 'Woodge'?

Positive options. The future. Geraldine's image continued to fade, until was little more than a visual echo, like the hand of the lady slipping back into the lake with the sword after King Arthur's last battle. No more conflict, Leo vowed. Chasing an English blue-stocking with all the alarums and excursions that entailed was too much, the rewards too few, the path too strewn with psychological Molotov cocktails. Besides, everything was preparing for fresh starts here. Of course, there would be miseries and weights from the past; but the very fact that things had been so bad could be an incentive now, couldn't it?

Here was potential. Here was youth. And here before them, as he led her through moonshine, was the Polonia Hotel.

He'd had her hand in his arm as if they'd been married for years. But in the lobby waiting for them was her last night's combatant, Andrzej; and the arm tensed.

'Would you like to get your key and go up?' Leo asked *sotto voce*, as if she'd just been some old dear he'd been helping to cross the street.

'My key?!' she asked, frigid, not getting it.

Rising from his chair, the boy started towards them. 'Your key,' Leo echoed, as if there were no doubt that they'd been booked into separate rooms.

'Ah!' she murmured, getting it now, and, turning to the desk, said 'Good evening' to Andrzej in passing.

'Evening,' he nodded, his gaze as inscrutable as when they'd been playing 'Murder' the night before. 'May I possibly have a word with you, sir?'

'So long as you don't call me that.'

'Call you what, sir?'

'Just that.'

Despatching Iwanka into the lift, he led Andrzej to the bar. There he heard a story that he might have dismissed as pure fantasy if it hadn't been this one of the merry troupe telling it:

He, Andrzej, had driven to Warsaw via Łódź. His contact there, Docent Gombrowicz, had already gone to work on the Geraldine Scott case. The facts were as follows: she had given a lecture at the Philological Institute two mornings before; later she'd gone to a performance of *Don Giovanni*; her driver had meanwhile been beaten up in the street. Discovering this, she had taken him to a university hostel in the woods to recover. The caretaker of the hostel had raised an alarm the following night when neither she nor the driver had reappeared as arranged. The directress of the Institute was rung, several other calls made, a search commenced; that was when the really fantastic had emerged. The driver's clothes had been found on a trail in the woods next to the track of a wild boar; two kilometres off, the naked body of a Kalmuk had turned up strangled; in a holiday shack in between a taxi-driver had appeared gagged and dressed in posh Englishman's hunting gear, which didn't fit; a stack of crates marked 'United Nations Relief' in Cyrillic had been sitting around him – they turned out to contain the latest in state-of-the-art Kalashnikov rifles manufactured by an ex-Warsaw Pact arms factory in Kazaniak, Bulgaria. Docent Gombrowicz had gleaned all this information from a *Solidarność* colleague in the Łódź police. He, the detective, had discovered that the gun-runners were led by one Vitaly Bazarov, a Russian living in a just-finished villa at the edge of the woods. Bazarov had an accomplice: a Polish young lady who until recently had been a lecturer herself at the Łódź Institute.

'Am I going too fast for you, sir?' Andrzej inquired.

'The name's Leo. It is pretty sensational, but I don't pretend to know your country. Let's cut to the chase, as your friend Mikoi might say. What's happened to Professor Scott?'

'That's the mystery. Nobody can find either her or the driver, though his Polski Fiat is still parked by the Grand Hotel. The Russian's done a bunk – apparently he and his girl and another woman left this morning in a silver Mercedes. Maybe the other woman was your friend, but why should she have gone with them? She may have met the girl at the literary conference in Kraków last week. The girl gave a paper on totalitarianism there. Gombrowicz says it was her last chance to redeem herself before the Institute decided whether to suspend her, but she blew it by making a manifestation about bringing back Communism.'

Oh Geraldine, Leo thought: what've you got into with your adventurism? Has some old leftish, ideological game led you into a nasty real world? Are you on your way to some silly posturing as British radical Woman-with-a-Cause? Have you been conned into thinking you're going to get relief supplies to some war zone? Do you fantasize, or half-wish, that you're going to be cast to play some media-role as a hostage? Is that what your ego craves now? more of the kind of self-aggrandizement which led you from me years ago? Or is this about sex? Is all the com-plicated cops-and-robbers business just some post-Commie, Eastern cover for the real truth: that you're off screwing some young Slavic rabbit somewhere? Either way, my darling, you're lost to me now. You've become a stranger, and I can no longer quite understand you.

'Sir?' Andrzej went on.

'Leo,' he corrected, a vacancy as of age coming into his eyes.

'Mikoi says we should keep trying. Is that right?'

'Trying?'

'To find her and keep our bargain with you.'

'Your bargain? Oh yes, if you like.'

The boy hesitated. 'It's not what we like, sir. She's your friend, not ours.'

'Yes, I suppose that is true.'

'Shall we change your plane reservation?'

'I guess I can't leave Poland till she's found now, can I?'

'I wouldn't have thought so. And if you're going to back us in our plan for a nightclub, we hope you won't leave that soon.'

The ritual of going to bed was played out with more formality than Leo was used to. When he arrived at the room, Iwanka was in the bath; she opened the door in a towel, then vanished back to elaborate ablutions. Tired, uncertain, he stripped to his shorts and got into the one of the flimsy twin beds nearest an alcove that led to windows and a view of the Palace of Kultur.

He thought about pushing the beds together but didn't. In his experience, women let you know when they wanted what; and apart from having allowed herself to be booked into the same room, Iwanka had given no overt sign. Doubtless she was eager not to appear easy; possibly she was calculating how to make him feel obliged. But if those weren't enough to encourage him to keep the furniture as it was, there was the familiar, intervening spectre of Geraldine Scott, which, following Andrzej's revelations, was now re-enshrouding him.

Agony is attractive, Leo reflected. The altar-pieces from the Museum re-entered his mind. Why was it so? Not for its beauty: it was ugly. Nor for its pleasure: it gave mostly pain. Only for its illusion of knowledge did it have positive value: a sharp twinge of it allowed you to imagine you'd 'been there'. Agony made for solidarity of a kind, Leo mused, stuck in his spiritual slough of despond. It allowed you to think you knew some of what others had suffered, and worse than yourself. For him, as for Poland, it was a kind of initiation. – Wasn't that why both of them had persisted in it for so long?

Semi-consciously, Leo had imagined for years that he was not worthy of a happy life. Despite his affectation of being content with himself, he'd clung to his evil, haunting iconness as if she were as close to fulfilment as he could get. He had hoped in his heart that, if agony *were* an initiation, she might be going through something similar too, one day to re-emerge into the light, chastened, ready for her original true lover again, like Psyche in the myth with Cupid. Leo had clung to this fantastic medallion as his lungs had been crushed gasping for air going down. Yet now, as he hugged its not all-discomforting shadow, a Polish woman was coming out of the bathroom towards him.

She was in a white nightdress with cheap but pretty Eastern lace on its bodice. Around her neck hung a crucifix: a small, simple statement perhaps of residual belief in chastity. Getting into the other one of the two beds, she switched out the lamp.

'Goodnight,' she breathed.

Then:

'I have asked the desk to phone us at six in the morning, so you will not miss your plane.'

'That's good.'

Silence.

'And thank you for a delicious dinner.'

'My pleasure.'

More silence.

'And for not exposing me in front of Andrzej.'

Leo almost smiled. 'That was my pleasure too.'

Beyond the cheap curtains, the red light on the spire of the Palace of Kultur blinked on and off.

'And it would be my pleasure even more to kiss you goodnight,' he added tentatively.

She did not answer. So, after a spell, he pulled back his covers and stepped over to her one of the flimsy twin beds.

Slipping under her covers, he put an arm around a waist and spooned himself against a body tauter and more alive than he'd known in years.

'I can't do this with you,' she protested. 'You must not. I do not want to get pregnant.'

'Don't you have any condoms?'

'Of course not. And I would not do that even if I did.'

'Why not? Everyone uses them nowadays.'

'Not here in Poland, not yet. At least not women like me.'

He tried a bit harder. Her legs were squeezed shut. At last, he rolled off in irritation.

'I'm sorry,' she said. 'But I try to be a good Catholic.'

'I understand.'

'And I do not want this with a man until I marry.'

Could such an attitude be genuine, in this day and age?

'I need to trust a man,' she concluded. 'And if I were pregnant, I would want him to be a good father.'

To be a good father – now there was a thought. He had been artfully dodging it for years. It was one more thing his obsession with Geraldine had helped him evade: one more respect in which his apparent attachment to life had been a sham. Really Leo had wanted to be a teenager forever: to have his cake and eat it too – that was the Western disease, wasn't it? And now he was trying to infect this Eastern female with it. Only Iwanka wouldn't let herself in for that kind of illness. Or would she?

Slowly, like depression, the thought came to him that her reluctance might be a sham too: a poor Easterner's 'method', a Slavic female's trick to entrap the rich Western man. Leo hoped this was not so; he found himself wishing to believe that, in their relative innocence, these people were still virtuous by and large and that, in exchange for material know-how, they might resurrect a ghost of virtue in decadent Westerners like himself. At some level, Leo might even have *liked* playing the rôle she apparently wished for him, as if a good Catholic, with full commitment. But could his type, ever? Hadn't his culture gone too far down the other path? Hadn't he been too slippery for too long, into deals and out of them so quickly that half of London thought of him as a wind-up artist in business as well as sex? 'Slick-willy stuff', as Geraldine used to call it. Still, his procedure had made him a success, hadn't it? But did he really want to behave like that here and now?

His body longed to roll on top of the woman's and force it. His mind told him to hold off and support the merry troupe: Mikoi and Andrzej, Monika and the rest. Why not back them to buy a whole street in Łódź or wherever? turn grim reminders of the nation's pain into places of cakes and ale? He might not even have to stump up his own cash to seed it: he could contact Norman's 'dentists' in Chicago – why not? It would be poetic justice to have *them* bankroll resurrection in a place their grandfathers had helped build, only to be thrown out of.

More thinking like this and I'm going to turn into a liberal Brit-with-a-Cause myself, Leo reflected. (Would *that* impress Geraldine enough to win her back?)

'What are you thinking?' Iwanka had meanwhile asked. 'Have I upset you? I'm sorry. I'm a virgin, you see.'

She had turned her face towards him. To his shock, Leo felt wet, hot tears on her cheek.

Like hunger and fear mixed, desire convulsed him. His middle-aged body seemed as if twenty again.

'I can't,' she protested. 'Please don't... please...'

When it was over, she wept silently. Meanwhile, Leo Hooper, exhausted, rolled onto his back. One of his arms dropped over the edge of the too-narrow bed. A knuckle hit on some little hard thing that moved. Turning on his side, he gazed down and, in the light through the curtains, made out a broken string of pearls.

— *London, 1993 and after*